Dodge City Public Library
Dodge City, Kansas

F(M) 832533

Russell, Martin

BACKLASH

Dodge City Public Library
Dodge City, Kansas

10001160
Dodge City Library

Backlash

MARTIN RUSSELL

Backlash

WALKER AND COMPANY
NEW YORK

Copyright © 1981 by Martin Russell

All rights reserved. No part of this book may be reproduced or transmitted in any form or by any means, electric or mechanical, including photocopying, recording, or by any information storage and retrieval system, without permission in writing from the Publisher.

All the characters and events portrayed in this story are fictitious.

First published in the United States of America in 1983 by the Walker Publishing Company, Inc.

ISBN: 0-8027-5493-7

Library of Congress Catalog Card Number: 82-51307

Printed in the United States of America

10 9 8 7 6 5 4 3 2 1

CHAPTER 1

When Albert telephoned at one-fifteen in the morning, I knew it had to be something serious. Albert was no night-owl. If he stayed up after eleven o'clock to watch the late movie he took care to mention the achievement the following day, as a mark of his manhood or something. A post-midnight call spelt trouble.

The tone of his voice supported the diagnosis.

'Steve? I'm sorry. It's Albert.'

'Yes, Albo?' The cretinous nickname had stuck to him with the tenacity of the household adhesive it reminded me of. 'What's the problem?'

'Did I get you out of bed?'

'No, I was finishing off some accounts. Something wrong?'

'I'm awfully sorry.' The words came across in jerks, as though being pumped with difficulty through the neck of a bottle. I wished he would stop apologizing. 'Could I possibly come round?'

'Here, you mean?'

'If I might. I'm terribly sorry if I'm disturbing you. I didn't know what else to do. I couldn't think of any other—'

'Drop in, by all means,' I told him. 'How long will you be?'

There was a pause. I thought perhaps he had silently rung off. 'Still there?' I asked. A faint yelp answered. 'Where are you ringing from?'

'I'm not sure . . .' He spoke hesitantly. 'North London, I think.'

'You *think*?'

'It must be somewhere in that region.'

'What are you doing there?'

'I'm in a call box.'

'I didn't imagine you were phoning from an underground sewer. Listen, Albo,' I said, with as much kindliness as I could muster in a cooling living-room in the desolation of the small hours after an evening's eye-crossing labour, 'if you want to come and see me, just get straight over here, will you? About half an hour?'

'It may take me longer than that.'

'Haven't you got the car?'

'Not with me.' He spoke as if he had left it in a cloakroom somewhere. 'I'll have to make my way as best I can.'

I sighed. 'I'll come over and pick you up. What's the number of that call box?' Vacancy greeted my question. 'Where is it located? You'll find the street name on the notice in front of you.'

He read it out, stumblingly and not too distinctly. It occurred to me that he had been drinking, and I started to brace myself against the explosion of another myth: that the Alberts of this world were incapable of kicking over the traces once in a while. As though sensing what was in my mind, he added on a note of defiance, 'I'm all right, you know, in myself. I mean, I'm not rambling. At least, I don't think so. It's just that I'm in a rather—'

'Stay right there,' I said resignedly. 'I'll be with you as soon as I can.'

The call box was empty.

Swearing to myself, I double-checked that it was the one Albert had described to me. Emerging, I glared in both directions along the forlorn street it stood in. Trust my partner, I thought, to fix a rendezvous and then carry out unilateral adjustments to the arrangement. It typified his approach to business. Nobody ever knew quite where they were with Albert. He confused people. It was simply part of his well-intentioned nature, and I had tried hard to condition myself to its quirks. But at two a.m., tolerance creaked a little. Crossing the pavement back to the car, I leaned through the open window and sounded the horn softly, twice.

Backing out again, I heard the scuff of a shoe.

In that instant, I knew I had walked into a trap. Entire revised versions of the action I should have taken danced through my mind, like the waking images of a dream. I was furious with myself. But committed. Before I could regain the car's protection, turn around, even, the blow would strike. My neck muscles tautened. I actually groaned in anticipation.

The groan that replied to mine was unmistakably Albertian, and twice as loud. And three times as prolonged. He loomed into my vision as I swung about, only to vanish again to my left. Completing my rotation, I saw that he had darted to the car's near side and was doubling his stringy frame into the passenger seat in a kind of cautious frenzy, spraying nervy glances into the gloom. Pursuing him inside, I put irritation into my slamming of the door, interrogation into my firing of the engine.

'Albert, what the bloody hell do you think you're—'

'Sorry, Steve,' he said mechanically. 'I didn't want to show myself.'

'You managed very well. Who are you hiding from?'

'No one in particular.'

'What the blazes have you been up to? Where's your car?'

He released what sounded like a sob. 'Mind if I tell you at home? I can't think straight.'

'*Your* home?'

'Sooner yours,' he said, low-voiced. 'If it's no trouble.'

On the brink of an ironical retort, I checked myself. A glance had shown me a sorry-looking Albert, a wreck of the man whom, ten hours previously, I had left at our office off Victoria Street, intoning letters into the audio for the later attentions of Amanda, our matchless secretary. At that time, neither his manner nor his appearance had given cause for alarm. Agitation of any kind, to be frank, was alien to the office when my partner was around. To see him as he was now was all the more jolting.

It would not be true to say he was dishevelled. His Tyrolean-style fur hat still clung to his narrow scalp like the limpet shell of a Brazil nut; his wool-lapelled suede coat engulfed him with its usual fidelity, open at the neck to display a traditional striped tie and a shirt collar of irreproachable Nile blue adhering rigidly to the upper contours of his thorax. The impression of collapse arose from something else. Instead of remaining upright in the seat, he seemed to be subsiding, imploding in slow-motion, as though under neutron bombardment which was altering his molecular structure. I said, less impatiently, 'Are you hurt at all? Were you mugged?'

His head shook.

'Where were you hiding yourself back there?'

'Some doorway,' he said vaguely. 'I thought I'd better stay out of sight.'

'Why?'

He offered no reply. I detected, I thought, a faint moaning from the region of his chest. 'Sure you're not hurt?'

'For God's sake,' he said. 'Can't you stop asking questions?'

I took a couple of deep breaths.

'It's a cold night,' I observed, 'in the middle of March. I've just driven ten miles at two in the morning to a forgotten street in Finchley to provide a taxi service for someone who would *seem* to be in trouble. I somehow think I'm entitled to a question or two. Don't apologize, Albo,' I added, finding top gear as we joined a main thoroughfare.

'I wasn't going to.'

'Just answer the question. Do you need medical attention?'

'I need advice.'

There was no more to be got out of him. Bowing to the inevitable, I gave attention to the navigation of London's night-softened arteries, alert to the menace of the occasional motorized antibody at intersections. Happily, the conditions were clear and dry, although now and then a gust seized the car and tried to send it the wrong way around a bollard. It was the kind of night that sounds better from inside a heated room: best of all, from between warm sheets. I thought yearningly of mine. The way things were going, I was in for a later bedtime than I had planned.

Albert followed me with a kind of stiff docility into the lift. When we emerged on the fifth floor he had still not uttered another syllable. The muteness persisted all the way to my apartment. Ushering him through to the living-room, I felt more than ever uneasy about his general deportment. It was so untypical. In my experience to date, Albert had been the ever-dependable guy, unfailingly and sometimes wearisomely up to the mark: his physical infallibility was something I had come to take for granted. Surely he wasn't about to flake out on me now? Pushing him down into the embrace of the deepest armchair, I headed for the drinks section of the built-in wall unit.

'Take the weight off your feet.' I kept my tone casual, trying to minimize the drama. High tension unsettles me. I'll sprint a mile to avoid it. 'Scotch or brandy?'

Getting no reply, I said, 'I'll make some coffee in a minute.' Pouring a measure of brandy, I took the glass across and planted it firmly on his limply upturned right palm. He sat staring ahead. With a sensation of mild panic—it was like having to deal with a fused robot—I removed his idiotic hat and transferred it to the nearby coffee table, where it sat in a hunched heap like a hibernating squirrel. He seemed barely aware of anything that I did.

Having examined him covertly for signs of external bruising—the mugging hypothesis remained front-runner—I went out to the kitchen. In the best of circumstances, I am not the finest host in London. Some have a flair for it: others know their limitations. In the teeth of intractable silence, I am a dead duck. I simply have no idea how to cope. Albert's muteness had unnerved me. From him, it was anything but what I was used to, and at two thirty in the morning I was short of inspiration for a means of breaking the deadlock.

In the event, no initiative was required from me. When I returned to the living-room with coffee he was standing with his back to the hi-fi panel, still clasping the brandy glass, gazing at me from his beanpole altitude with an expression of sheer misery.

He said, 'You've got to tell me what to do.'

'Okay,' I said reasonably, setting down the tray. 'What about?'

'The mess I'm in.'

'Do my best, if you'll tell me about it.'

'I don't know how to start.'

'Well, you know what they say.'

He looked at me as though I had spoken half a dozen words in Farsi. 'What?'

'Start at the beginning and go on from there.' He looked vacant. Soothingly I added, 'Imagine you're dictating an office memo. There's something you want to make clear to somebody else. How would you set about it?'

'We're not at the office.'

'No. But the principle applies.' A nightmarish quality of surrealism was creeping into the conversation. Everything I said seemed to take us further from the point.

'Come over here and park yourself again,' I suggested. 'Take a sip or two of this. Marshal your thoughts.'

'They're a congealed mass already.' A short, despairing laugh spouted from him. 'I can't tear one from another.'

He folded himself jerkily back into the armchair, began stirring his unsweetened coffee with an intent abstraction. 'All I do know is,' he said, almost calmly, 'it's the worst night of my life.'

My own view of it was starting to take a similar turn. With difficulty, I kept the bulk of the exasperation out of my voice.

'I can't help you unless I know what it is you're up against. Can I? Now, wouldn't it be a good idea if you told me, first of all, how you spent the earlier part of the evening . . . where you went, what you did? Can't we kick off from there?'

I studied him hopefully. He was regarding me with a slight frown, as though assessing the validity of my suggestion. For fully a minute he said nothing. I began seriously to wonder whether he was dead drunk. I had never seen him tight, or even tipsy; I knew nothing of alcohol's effect upon him; perhaps it took him this way, a stiff-limbed paralysis of judgement, a descent into unreasoning horror. About to put yet another prodding question, I stopped as he spoke again.

'The early part of the evening doesn't matter. It's what happened at the end.'

I nodded with what I hoped was an air of scholarly attentiveness. 'What did happen?'

He looked at me over the coffee cup. 'I think I've killed somebody.'

CHAPTER 2

I made him tell me from the beginning.

Once launched, he kept fairly well to the track, and the further he went the steadier his progress. In evident anxiety to set the circumstances squarely before me he went meticulously into detail, which explains my ability to reproduce his account in narrative style . . . the best way, I think, to convey its flavour as well as its sense. Although I am relying on memory, overall accuracy is guaranteed. I may have slipped up on a point or two, but nothing of significance.

Albert's Story—One

The applause for the soloist was thunderous.

Albert contributed his share. The person to his right supplied more than hers: so wholehearted was her clapping that she lost her programme. Groping beneath the seats, he retrieved it for her.

Thanking him with a gesture, she continued to clap. The soloist, small, neat, humble, returned for the fourth time to become the recipient of an immense floral sheaf and a standing ovation. On her fifth disappearance the house lights went up. In a buzz of discussion, elements of the audience made for the bars.

Albert resumed his seat.

The person to his right did the same. While they were upright, he had received an impression of average stature and an easy stance, although, intent upon platform events, he had given her only marginal attention until the hubbub had dwindled and they were left in relative isolation in the ninth row of the grand tier, watching the removal of the piano from the hall. At that juncture, he eyed her sideways.

She seemed oblivious of him. With the programme spread upon her knees, she was reading the potted biography of the pianist with apparent absorption. Albert couldn't help noticing her hands. They were small and well-modelled, artistic hands, the type he had always admired; they would not, he thought, have disgraced the pianist herself. In all probability he was sitting alongside an aspirant to the concert platform. It was this reflection, as much as anything, that prompted his overture.

'She can certainly play, can't she?'

The girl—he estimated her age at something under thirty—made a half-response with a smile and a nod, and continued to read. The fact that she had neither ignored him nor replied with excessive politeness emboldened Albert.

'Odd,' he remarked, consulting his own programme, 'how the Asians seem to be outdoing us at our own culture. Either it says a lot for their dedication or it doesn't say much for ours.'

'According to this, she's Egyptian.'

'They're Eastern, aren't they? Getting on that way. Fact remains, whether they hail from Korea or the sands of the Kalahari, they all seem to have more . . more *application* than us decadent Westerners, a greater aptitude for—'

'Surely there are heaps of good European pianists?'

'A number,' he agreed promptly. He was pleased to note that she had removed her gaze from the programme to give him steady-eyed appraisal. Her expression was pleasant, if reserved. Her dark hair was set in a bouffant style that, even to Albert, seemed a trifle dated; and yet it was not ill-suited to her personality. Weighing her up, he lost the thread of his argument. 'I'm really talking about the . . . you know . . . the ultimate spark, the sort of radiance that can, you know . . .'

'You mean, with the Europeans it's all technique and no soul?'

'Exactly!' Albert was thrilled. 'Take an example. This young fellow who's just won first prize in the Kadetzki . . ." He paused. 'Look here, we could chat a lot more comfortably in the bar, don't you think?'

'Pardon?'

'Over a drink. Would you care for something?'

The girl glanced down at her programme, then at the platform. 'Now, you mean?'

'Why not?' said Albert, puzzled.

She hesitated. 'I'd quite like a drink, actually. All right. It's very kind of you.'

The bar resembled a shoe shop at Sale time. Leaving the girl against a wall by a mirror, Albert joined the battalions that were laying siege to the bartenders. As time passed, desperation ate into him. He was convinced that she would lose patience, return alone to her seat; and it was suddenly important to him that she should do nothing of the kind. When eventually he emerged from the ruck with a glass in each hand, he was gratified and yet astonished to find her still there, regarding him gravely as he apologized his way back to her.

'Worse than an East End pub,' he observed, reaching her side. 'Orange juice, you said?'

'Grapefruit, actually. It doesn't matter. You must have had a frightful struggle to catch someone's eye.'

'I'll take it back and—'

'No, really. This is lovely. I'm so thirsty.'

Albert sucked at his lager. 'With an hour of Bruckner to come, something had to be done about that. Trouble with these places, you can't get a decent drink in civilized conditions. It's all pandemonium. Probably the best thing is to bring a flask or something. I never think of it. By the way, I forgot to ask your name.'

She looked across at two small men who were arguing about Mozart. 'Ross,' she said, after a moment. 'Jennifer Ross.'

'Albert Hall.'

'Pardon?'

'Some people call me Albo. I've always felt . . .' He paused as she choked into her drink. 'Are you all right, Jennifer?'

Crimson-faced, she turned away to cough. 'Sorry. Yes, I'm fine.' She coughed again. 'You must forgive me. It took me unawares.'

Albert smiled thinly. 'You're referring to my name? It does affect some people that way.'

He took a lengthy pull at his lager. Jennifer placed her empty glass carefully on the shelf below the mirror.

'Hearing it in this particular environment . . .'

Draining his glass, Albert added it to hers on the shelf. He said nothing.

Jennifer seemed to lose her remaining poise. 'I didn't mean to cause you any—'

'I don't honestly mind,' he said stiffly. 'It's quite funny, isn't it? My father had an unusual sense of humour.'

'I'm sure he wouldn't have wanted you to—'

'I was saying, this lad who's just walked off with the top award in the Kadetzki Memorial Competition, well, I heard him a week or two ago, playing the Schumann with the L.P.O. under Casper, and really, listening to him . . . Of course, relatively he's still a novice. One allows for that. Even so, the impression I had, listening to him . . . Here's a young hopeful, I remember thinking, who can hit all the right notes when he has to, who can give you the *structure* of the work, but what does it add up to? Where's the *poetry*?'

'But then, as you say, he's young.' There was a faraway look in Jennifer's eyes.

'How old's this Egyptian? Nineteen?'

'I must admit, she was very good.'

Albert peered at the shelf. 'Shall I try and get you another of those?'

'There wouldn't be time,' she said, fiddling with the top button of her dark red cardigan. Albert had a soft spot for cardigans. They tended, in his view, to enhance femininity. Jennifer's figure, he had already noted, was of the boyish variety; and again, it seemed entirely in character. Below the cardigan she wore a black skirt with a pleat at the rear, and a pair of shiny white plastic boots whose length he could only guess at, since they vanished beneath the skirt. A silver bangle encircled her left wrist. While he was trying covertly to examine the fingers of her left hand, the end-of-interval gong began to intone. Jennifer looked up at him, and caught him looking down.

He said hurriedly, 'Perhaps we ought to be drifting back.'

She moved towards the exit. He kept pace with her left elbow. 'Take you long to get here?'

'Not too bad,' she said over her shoulder. 'A ride on the Tube, then a bus along.'

'You don't run a car?'

'I could borrow my father's. Parking's such a problem, though. I find it more restful to leave the car at home.'

'They could use you,' Albert said waggishly, 'on the buses.'

'Pardon?'

'Jennifer Ross says, "Ride and Relax with London Transport".'

'Oh.' She looked and sounded blank. 'Yes.'

Back in their seats, they sat in silence for a few moments, watching the orchestra return in apathetic fragments to the platform. Presently Albert shaded his eyes.

'They're a bit light,' he said worriedly, 'on the brass. Hope we're not in for a skimped performance.'

Jennifer rearranged her coat across her knees. 'You seem to know a lot about music.'

'Not really,' he said modestly.

'Do you play an instrument?'

'I went to Grade Five on the clarinet.'

'How marvellous.'

Albert shifted uneasily. 'Probably sounds more than it was. There were twenty grades in that class, and it was for nine-year-old beginners.'

'What made you give it up?' she asked, after a pause.

'Chickenpox.'

'You must have had it badly.'

'Not me. The teacher. She was only a kid.'

'Oh.'

'By the time she'd lost her spots, I'd lost interest. Or my parents had.'

They rose to allow some people to pass to their seats. When they were reinstated, Jennifer said, 'I often wish I could play something. One feels so useless without a skill.'

Albert seized his chance. 'What do you do, Jennifer?'

Her head jerked round. 'For a living, you mean? I design dresses.'

'My,' he said tolerantly. Moments passed while he thought about it. 'Make your own clothes?'

She shook her head. 'I'm afraid I buy them off the peg. By the time I get home, I've usually had quite enough of cutting and shaping.'

'Yes, I can understand that. I'm the same, rather.' She said nothing. She was observing the arrival of the second violins. 'As an accountant,' he explained, 'I find that people are apt to say Aha! You must be sitting pretty, bet you fiddle your income tax . . . when the fact of the matter is, figure-work is something I detest. Can't stand it. In fact, I pass my tax returns on to a friend of mine, who makes a damn sight better job of it than I would. In exchange, I service his car.'

Jennifer looked up with a glint of interest. 'And I suppose he's a mechanic?'

'No. As a matter of fact he works in a bank.'

'If you don't like figures,' she said, studying the percussionist, 'whatever made you become an accountant?'

'Oh, well. You know how it is. We've always been a bit bookish in our family. I was fairly set on something in the engineering line, but my people . . . Anyhow, I did the five-year grind, or was it six? . . . can't recall . . . must have been six, because I remember my people saying . . . anyhow, I managed to get chartered. I'd fluff the exams now.'

'Still, once you're a C.A. I suppose you can land a job practically anywhere?'

'It helps. Getting back to dressmaking, are you by any chance one of these people who design these quite incredible—'

'Nothing like that,' she said firmly. 'I'm with a firm that supplies one of the big chain stores. Quite dreary, actually.'

The conductor appeared. The house lights dimmed. Albert sat rigid, conscious of Jennifer's profile in the dusk.

Albert's Story—Two

'Say what you like about Bruckner, the old boy had scale.'

'How do you mean?'

'Well, he was able to conjure up these moments of epic grandeur between what some people might regard as expanses of motiveless aridity, despite which—'

'His symphonies are so huge,' said Jennifer.

Albert took her up keenly. 'You'd argue that what he has to say could be stated within the limits of a narrower compass?'

'I just think they go on too long.'

Jennifer's gaze drifted off to roam the coffee-bar. A trio of coloured youths were chatting up the girl on duty; they were the only other inhabitants of the place. Outside, traffic powered its way along Kensington High Street. Scraps of rubbish sailed past in the breeze.

Albert frowned into his beaker. 'Don't you feel, though, this could have been deliberate policy on Bruckner's part? Periods of understatement, then . . . wham!'

She gave him a look across the table. 'Why not just keep in the good parts?'

'Force of contrast.'

She shrugged. 'I find it tedious.'

'Do you really?'

Silence settled between them. Jennifer took some rapid sips of coffee, eyeing the street. The black woolly coat she was now wearing went rather happily, in Albert's estimation, with the white boots.

He took a leaflet from his inside pocket. 'There's another concert by the same crowd on the twenty-first.'

She put down the beaker. 'You go to a lot of concerts?'

'Not as many as I'd like. You?'

'If a spare ticket comes up at the firm.'

Albert blinked. 'You get buckshee ones?'

'Just occasionally.'

'Very nice too. I suppose you have to take your turn. I was wondering . . .'

She looked at him enquiringly. He stuttered a little. 'You wouldn't c-care to come along on the twenty-first?'

Back into her eyes crept the faraway look. 'I don't think I'm free. My father's taking me out to dinner that day.'

Albert feigned a friendly interest. 'Special occasion?'

'Birthday.'

'That'll be nice. Hope it, er, goes off well. Your parents must think a lot of you.'

'Just my father,' she explained. 'Mother's dead.'

'I'm sorry. You look after your dad?'

'Do my best.'

Albert surveyed her with avuncular gravity. 'Ever take him to a concert? Or doesn't he care for music?'

Her fingers tightened on the beaker's handle. 'There was only the one ticket for tonight. He said I might as well use it.'

'Well now, look here.' Albert spoke expansively. 'I've enjoyed your company this evening, Jennifer. Really appreciated it. I'd like to repay. How would it be if I got seats for some other concert and we all three went along to celebrate your birthday?'

'I don't think . . .' She looked confused. 'He's not ever so keen on music, actually.'

'Skip that idea, then. Come with me by yourself.'

'It's awfully kind of you.' She took some more rapid sips.

He dug into another pocket. 'I've a monthly schedule here somewhere . . .'

'I can't make Tuesdays or Thursdays.'

'Tuesdays and Thursdays *out*—okay. What have we?' He peered down the list. 'Brahms's Second Piano Concerto, April three, a Wednesday, how would that be? Rachmaninov Number Three, two days later, Friday . . .'

'I'm not sure about Brahms. Or Rachmaninov, for that matter.'

'There's a Viennese Night, the following Sunday.'

'I always think they're a bit tiresome. Those choppy selections.'

'I'm inclined to agree. No sooner does one piece—'

'Anyhow, I couldn't make Sunday.'

'Not Sunday?'

'Not the weekends at all, actually.' Her brown eyes conned him seriously. 'I prefer to keep them free. For my father.'

More desultorily, Albert's forefinger pursued the list to

the foot of the page. 'The choice elsewhere's rather limited next month. There's Webern and Bartok on the twenty-second . . .'

'Oh, my.'

'That about exhausts the possibilities.'

'It's really nice of you to go to all this bother. What a pity there's nothing.'

Albert assured her it was no bother. 'I'm frankly keen to repeat a very pleasant evening. Another coffee, Jennifer?'

'No, thanks awfully. I'll have to be off.'

'Hang on a bit,' Albert said, alarmed. 'We've nothing fixed. There must be something here that would suit us both.'

She began putting on her gloves. 'Perhaps we'd better leave it for next month.'

'Which are you more dubious about, Brahms or Rachmaninov?'

'It's not a terribly good time for me,' she said, shouldering her bag. 'I'm a bit tied up for a while.'

Rising as she pushed back her chair, he hastened round to tug it clear of her path. 'It might be nice to just meet up again for coffee and a chat. You know.' Inspiration crashed into him. 'Or a meal somewhere. We don't have to listen to music.'

'I cook for my father,' she said slowly. 'So it's a little awkward.'

'What is?'

'Going out to meals.'

'Bring him along,' exclaimed Albert.

'He's rather a stick-in-the-mud. Prefers home cooking.'

Albert said teasingly, 'He's taking you out to dinner on the twenty-first.'

'Good night,' Jennifer said to the girl on duty, who failed to hear. On the pavement, in the teeth of the wind, she added, 'That's a very special occasion. He couldn't think what to buy me for my birthday, so . . .'

Albert inhaled a gulp or two of the frigid air. 'Jennifer, I'd very much like to see you again. Isn't there some way we can arrange it?'

She started walking, holding the lapels of her coat across her throat. 'I expect we'll run into each other at the hall again some time.'

'That's too indefinite,' he said urgently, matching her strides. 'I'd like to feel . . . Well, now that we're acquainted, I'd be very sorry indeed to lose touch with you.'

'We'd better hurry,' she said. 'My father starts to panic if I'm late.'

Albert took pride in his handling of a car in urban conditions. His technique was to talk fluently of unrelated things while coping dispassionately with the traffic swirls and eddies in a way that was calculated to saturate his passengers with the cool confidence that he considered them entitled to. He did it to me once, and I never drove with him again.

'After that,' he told Hyde Park Corner, 'I moved on to this rival outfit who were offering more. But inside a week I found I'd taken the wrong step. So I left there, scouted round a bit. There wasn't much doing just at the—'

Jennifer gave a little shriek. 'Did you see that taxi? He nearly took your wing off.'

'Finally, this buddy of mine came along with a proposition. It seemed to have possibilities. So I went in with him, and we clicked. My goodness, did we click. It was around the start of the property boom, and we—'

'Property,' she said, colourlessly.

'Know something about it?'

'Nothing reputable.'

'There's a legitimate side to it, you know,' Albert said earnestly. 'For those willing to accept a degree of risk, the rewards can be—'

'Left here for the station.'
'Nonsense. I'm driving you home.'
'Certainly not.'
'It's no trouble.'
'You're not to dream of it.'
'I'm not dreaming. I'm doing it. Talk me along the route.'

Getting no response, he flicked her a glance which all but cost him his no-claim bonus. When the tyres had stopped screaming and he was back on course he looked at her again. She was biting her lip.

'Please,' she said quietly, 'take me to the station.'

'All right, Jenny. I was only kidding. I'll dump you on the Tube if that's what you prefer.'

'My name's Jennifer.'

'Sorry. It slipped out. Suits you, somehow.' Plunging into the whirlpool of Marble Arch, he allowed the main current to carry them to the far side. 'Doesn't anyone call you Jenny?'

Slewing the car to the right, he brought it to a bucking standstill on virgin asphalt beneath the main legs of the Arch. Jennifer glanced about her, nonplussed. Albert contorted in his seat to face her.

'It was presumptuous of me, I suppose. I just have this feeling I've . . . come to know you. We seem to hit the same waveband. Is that how you feel?'

'A question of that sort,' she said tightly, 'shouldn't need to be asked.'

'No,' he said, impressed. 'Good point. Well, I suppose I'd better let you go and catch your train. If you walk over there to the steps it'll take you down to the ticket barrier. Before you go, though . . .'

She had the door open and was scrambling out. He said, 'Hang on a second, Jennifer.'

Her face came back. 'Thank you for the drinks, and the lift. It was most kind of you. 'Bye.'

'Hey! Wait a bit.'

By the time he had forced his interminable legs out of the car she was midway across the open space on course for the subway. 'Jennifer!' he shouted desperately. 'We haven't fixed anything. I shan't know where to . . . Oh, Christ.'

He glanced back at the car. When his gaze switched again, she was almost out of view down the steps. With a frantic kick at a tyre, he went after her.

Crowded though the train was, he managed to find a seat opposite hers. Her lips tightened as she watched him settle.

'By the time you get back, your car will have been towed away.'

'To hell with the car,' said Albert.

'Don't be absurd. It's all so unnecessary. You didn't have to follow me on to the train.'

'I didn't?'

Every phrase had to be bawled above the bellow of the wheels.

'We left it that we'd probably meet again at another concert.'

'That's supposed to lift my adrenalin?' he demanded. 'Chances are we'd never set eyes on each other again, and you know it.

'We never had set eyes on each other before tonight.'

'So I didn't miss you, did I? It's different now.'

She looked through the window at the hurtling walls of the tunnel. 'I don't believe in these instant . . . friendships.'

'You consider that a relationship has to grow, unfold?'

'Yes, of course.'

'So how,' he asked triumphantly, 'does it ever grow, if it's nipped in the bud?'

Jennifer glanced nervously to her left. The middle-aged

man sitting beside her was apparently engrossed by his evening paper. The woman next to Albert was gazing into space. Leaning forward, Albert propped his right elbow on a knee and cupped his face with a hand.

'Listen, Jennifer. I'll tell you something. I've always had this vague hope that something like tonight might happen. Now that it has . . . I'm not casual about these things. Don't get the wrong idea. But someone has to open the batting. Someone has to talk. Then, if matters develop . . .' He gulped and swallowed. 'I'm not trying to give a crash course on social relationships. I'm merely trying to account for my persistence—because it's not my nature, you know. Normally I give up fairly easily. But something about the way we were thrown together . . . I feel it would be such an awful waste if we can't manage to arrange another date.'

'We've tried, and we can't. So that's an end of the matter, isn't it?'

He gazed at her for a moment. 'You're content to let it slide, just like that?'

'I don't see the need to make an issue of it.' She inclined forward in her turn, so that their foreheads were three inches apart. 'Do you realize that technically you're molesting me?'

'Don't be ridiculous.'

'I'm going to change seats,' she informed him.

'What for?'

'If it's not obvious, I can't make it any plainer.'

'I shall move with you.'

'If you do, I shall ask for help. I'm warning you. It will all be highly embarrassing.'

'I've every bit as much right to be on this train as you have.'

'Certainly,' she agreed, rising. 'But if you want my candid advice . . .'

The head of the man next to her swung upwards from

the racing page; his protuberant eyes clamped themselves upon her. She stopped again.

'If I were you,' she murmured into Albert's right ear, 'I'd get out at the next station, catch the next train back to Marble Arch, collect your car, pay the fine, go home and forget you ever saw me. Is that understood? Good night, then, and thank you again. I really did enjoy our chat,' she added on a formal note. 'Excuse me.'

With a smile at their fellow passengers, now nakedly staring, she stepped between their knees and turned to her left, making her way unsteadily but purposefully to the farther end of the car. Albert sat motionless, watching her as she found another seat.

Albert's Story—Three

'Do you want me to call the police?'

Albert said stubbornly, 'I simply don't believe you'd do such a thing.'

'Try me.' Her voice quivered. 'Or rather, don't. You might find yourself in a much stickier position than you'd bargained on.'

'It can hardly be much worse than it is,' he retorted. 'Aren't you going to open the door?'

'Not with you standing here.' Withdrawing the key from the lock, she turned to face him challengingly. 'Why did you follow me home?'

'Couldn't help it. I had to know where you lived.'

'Well, now that you know, kindly leave me in peace. I don't like being tailed through the streets—especially at night. I never heard of such a thing.'

'I surprised myself a bit,' he admitted.

'Are you leaving?'

'Not without some guarantee from you.'

'What on earth are you talking about?'

'Some assurance,' Albert said loudly, 'that you don't intend just to pass out of my life without giving an instant's thought to the—'

'Shhhh!' She glanced apprehensively at the upper windows of the block. 'You'll wake the neighbourhood. For heaven's sake, come inside a minute.'

He followed her into a miniature hallway, bare of furniture or fitments, that led through to an L-shaped living-room on two levels, the foot of the L being two steps above the remainder. Snapping on lights, Jennifer advanced to a dresser, dumped her bag, turned to confront him.

'Shut the door,' she ordered. He complied. 'Are you satisfied now? You should be. You've not only tracked me to my lair, you've managed to invade it, I don't quite know how. Now listen. I'm only going to say this once. Are you paying attention?'

Albert nodded. 'I'm listening hard.'

'The easiest thing,' she said slowly, 'would be for me to agree to meet you again some time, get rid of you that way for tonight. But it wouldn't be fair. I've no intention of meeting you again: I want that straight from the start. You know my address now, there's nothing to be done about that. But I warn you. If you try, just try, making use of the knowledge after tonight, I shall have no hesitation in getting you dealt with by the proper authorities. Do I make myself clear?'

'It seems to me an utterly ludicrous—'

'Please keep your voice down. You'll disturb my father.'

Albert resumed in a fierce whisper. 'Anyone might think I'd just crept up on you out of the gutter. An hour or two ago we were chatting over coffee. Now, suddenly—'

'We've gone beyond that. Don't you see?'

There was a gentler note to her voice. She stood leaning against the dresser, studying him. Presently she said, 'Before you go, would you like another cup of coffee?

You'll have quite a journey back.'

'Thank you,' he said tonelessly. 'I think I would.'

'Park yourself over there.'

Removing her coat, she dropped it on to a studio couch against the wall, opened a door and disappeared from his sightline. A rattling of china commenced. From his chair at the foot of the steps leading to the floor's higher level, Albert broodingly surveyed the room. Agreeably proportioned, it was decorated with taste in pale gold wallpaper and faintly purplish paintwork, a little chipped here and there. The furniture, a few modern pieces, stood on wall-to-wall carpeting in a neutral shade, centrally enhanced by an oval rug in mottled gold and bronze. In the corner beyond the couch sat a record-player. A scattering of books and magazines occupied the shelves of a wall unit on the opposite side, the remaining sections being devoted to ornaments, quaint nodding figures, writing materials, a wooden bowl containing fruit, and three or four framed photographs, one of them showing a group in which a younger but instantly recognizable Jennifer was sandwiched between an older couple and a teenaged boy, with a tortoiseshell cat at foot level stalking out of the picture. Another photograph was that of a serious-faced young man in Air Force uniform bearing pilot's wings. Albert eyed it morosely.

'It's true what I said, you know,' he called.

'What? Please don't shout.'

He lowered his voice. 'About you being the kind of person I've always wanted to run into.'

During the ensuing silence he pondered the photograph again. The pilot's wings stood out sharply, as though freshly sewn to the uniform. A suggestion of priggish complacency hovered at the corners of the young man's mouth.

Jennifer reappeared with a tray. Setting it on a low table alongside Albert's chair, she poised herself above it.

'White?' She poured from twin jugs. 'Help yourself to sugar. Rich tea biscuits or shortcakes. You'd better eat something. You might find the car gone when you get back.'

Albert said something dismissive about the car.

'That's a silly attitude.' Pouring another cup, she sat on the edge of the couch. 'You'll regret it tomorrow.'

He stared across at her. 'There's only one thing I'm likely to regret tomorrow.'

'Better a disappointment now,' she said briskly, 'than heartache later.'

'The heartache's here now.'

'Don't be idiotic. You hardly know me.'

'That's just it. I'd like to, but you won't let me.'

She looked down at the carpet. 'What's the use?'

Albert cleared his throat painfully. 'You've got someone already. Is this what you're trying to tell me?'

'I've got my father.' She was still looking at the floor.

'Is he an invalid or something?'

'It's none of your business. He relies on me, that's all. I can't let him down.'

'In other words, you're prepared to devote your life to him?'

She said quietly, 'You can draw whatever conclusion you like.'

Replacing his cup on the tray, Albert drew breath. 'Tell me something, Jenny. If it weren't for this dad of yours, would you have agreed to see me again?'

She hesitated. 'That's a hypothetical question. I can't answer it.'

'Try.'

'Why should I?' she demanded. 'I don't owe you anything at all.'

'Not even an explanation?'

Her cup and saucer swooped to the floor. Jumping up, she stalked angrily across to the wall unit and buttressed herself by an elbow against an upper shelf, with the other hand on her hip. She gazed down at him with a kind of disbelief.

'An *explanation?*' Her head shook wonderingly. 'Do you know, you're a most extraordinary man? I've never met anyone quite like you. On the strength of one single soft drink in a concert interval, you seem to imagine I should be crawling at your feet. I shall scream in a minute.'

'And wake your father?' Albert said sarcastically. 'We can't allow that. How long have you been looking after him like this?'

'If you must know,' she said breathlessly, 'since my mother died.'

'You support him?'

'As best I can. Anything else I can tell you?'

'Only the name of his sleeping pills. With all this going on outside my bedroom door, I'd have been wide awake long ago.'

'I'm glad you realize it. He probably is. Now will you please finish your coffee and leave?'

'Okay,' Albert said equably. 'Sure.'

In a casual movement he rose and walked to the centre of the room. To his right was the half-open kitchen door; to his left, another door, tight shut. He nodded towards it. 'That where your dad sleeps?'

'Yes,' she said shortly.

In the same nonchalant manner he approached the door. She stiffened. 'What are you doing? Keep away from—'

Grasping the handle, he flung the door wide.

The room contained a bed, neatly made up, and empty. Nearby stood a dressing-table. On its walnut surface was ranged an assortment of bottles: cologne, face cream, talcum powder. A fluffy pink dressing-gown was draped over a chair, beneath which stood a pair of silver backless slippers.

For a few moments Albert stood looking. Closing the door at last, he returned to the central rug of the living-room. From her position near the wall, Jennifer watched him.

'Satisfied?'

'Puzzled.' Albert spoke reasonably. 'More than a little bewildered, Jenny, in fact. Why did you make him up?'

'You really want me to tell you?'

'It's why I'm asking.'

She shrugged. 'I didn't make him up. He does exist. Occasionally he sleeps here, when he comes to visit.'

'Oh. He visits you?'

'Not often. Mostly I'm on my own.' She paused. 'I like to be independent.'

'I'd noticed.'

'Don't you?' she asked.

'To an extent. Don't we all?'

'Then you should understand if I try to explain . . .'

Albert went and occupied her former place on the couch. 'Carry on. I'm listening.'

'It's not easy,' she said, haltingly.

Stooping, she began to fumble with things on the tray, altering their positions. 'I said I'm independent and it's true, but that doesn't mean . . . It doesn't mean I don't need company. Everybody does. It's purely a matter of when, and how much. Take yourself. You say you've been concert-going a lot, hoping to meet someone. That makes sense to me. I know the feeling.'

Albert stared. 'Then you must know what it means to me.'

She turned her face away. 'This is why I invented my father's reliance on me. I . . . didn't want you to get drawn in, and then hurt.'

'Why should I get hurt?'

'When you found that things weren't all you'd hoped.'

'Surely that's for me to decide. I don't get it. You go alone to a concert, you accept my invitation to a drink—'

'That,' she said tautly, 'is all it was. Just an interval drink in the bar.'

'Plus coffee afterwards. Don't forget that.'

'I'm forgetting nothing.' Her eyes closed for a second. 'It was quite a thrill for me, to be asked. If you want to know, I'd been half-hoping for something of the kind to occur. Yes, it's true. I don't . . .'

She paused again, fingering the sugar-bowl like a blind woman striving to read Braille. 'I'm not sure if you'd call me a lonely person. I'm not completely sure what loneliness is. I do know that if it's worse than the feeling I sometimes get, then I can understand people leaping from heights to blot it out.' The sugar-bowl overturned. She regarded the spilt grains vacantly. 'Music's quite good, of course. A consolation. But then, there's afterwards. All those quiet, peaceful restaurants where you can have a table to yourself and no one interferes with you, no one tries to intrude . . .'

Albert thrust a hand through his hair. 'You do know all about it, then.'

She began scooping up sugar with a teaspoon. 'I know enough.'

'This evening could have put a stop to all that. For both of us.'

She nodded slowly. 'It could.'

'Only you turned your back on it. Decided to opt for your precious independence. Is this what you're saying?'

'It'll do.'

Getting to his feet, Albert paced to the steps and back. 'Are you frigid, Jennifer?'

She flushed scarlet. 'Please don't talk like that.'

'In the circumstances,' he said warmly, 'I'll talk how I damn well please. It's false pretences, you know. Oh, yes. I've met girls like you before. On with the make-up, the bright smiles, the pleasing graces . . . then, the moment they're invited to dabble a toe, fadeout. No intention of committing themselves. They're cold. They know it. They know perfectly well they're incapable of a response, and yet despite that awareness—'

'Please stop.'

'Females like you, they don't even consider the other party. All they can think of is proving something to themselves. Trying to demonstrate they're up to scratch, when the brutal truth—'

'There's nothing I need to prove.' Once more the sugar-bowl somersaulted as she straightened up in agitation. 'I don't have to justify my conduct tonight. Not to you, not to anybody. Given the right . . .'

She halted. Her breathing was uneven. Albert frowned.

'The right what?'

'Forget it. Please go.'

Albert said, 'I'm not entirely a fool, you know.'

'No one's saying you are.'

'But you'd sooner meet someone like that, possibly? Someone with more sex appeal than sense?'

'I really think you'd better go.'

'I've a couple more things to say first. Now that we've reached this stage,' Albert said, with dignity, 'I feel I should speak my mind. Some other poor chump might benefit. You know what I think? In fairness to all, girls like you should retire to convents and stay out of people's hair. You're not fit to be on the loose. It's not right that you should be made available to the general—'

Collapsing into a chair, Jennifer covered her face and began to shake uncontrollably.

Albert studied her anxiously, wondering if he had gone too far. 'Look here,' he said awkwardly, 'I'm most terribly sorry. I didn't mean to upset you. Please don't cry.'

Her hands slid aside, revealing a face that was crimson and contorted, and tearless. 'Crying?' she panted. 'Who wants to cry? I'm nearly exploding with laughter. If you could only *hear* yourself!'

Albert gazed at her dumbly.

'You're worse even than I thought.' She shook her head, marvelling. 'I had you categorized as a stuffy, self-centred bore. Now it turns out you're bigoted into the bargain. Oh, my! A chauvinistic misfit.'

'Thank you. I'm most interested to hear that.'

'You're welcome.'

'Tell me one thing. How long did it take you to arrive at your earlier conclusion?'

Jennifer contemplated the wall. 'About eighteen minutes,' she said, and burst once more into helpless mirth.

'*Eighteen* minutes?'

'The length of the concert interval.' Springing up, she walked across to her bag, found a handkerchief, wiped her eyes. She turned to regard him with a cold smile. 'When you first spoke to me, I'll admit, I had hopes. They didn't last long.'

Albert found it hard to move his lips. 'Apparently,' he mumbled, 'they hung around long enough to let me buy you coffee afterwards.'

'You were very insistent,' she pointed out. 'You wouldn't take no then, just as you're refusing to accept it now. I shouldn't have weakened, but I did. I'm sorry. Obviously it gave you false ideas. But for heaven's sake, haven't I done my best ever since to repair the damage? If you can't take a hint when it's dropped on your foot, you'll have to put up with the agony.'

She was no longer smiling. She sounded fatigued. 'I'll give it one more try. This isn't a hint: it's a statement. You're tedious, Mr Albert Hall. Does that get through to you? You're a would-be middle-class shallow intellectual without the brains to suspect when you're boring a girl into a trance. There's one entertaining thing about you, and that's your name. And even that joke drops dead in your fist. There's a kind of . . . dull arrogance about you. It's unbelievable.'

She stood examining him with a certain curiosity. 'Can you really have got this far through life without tumbling to a thing or two? Yes, I believe you have. I believe you're genuinely in the dark. I'm being blunt. I have to be. With you, it seems to be the only way.'

Returning for the tray, she carried it towards the kitchen door. Across a shoulder she said, 'If you'll excuse me now, I must get to bed or I'll never make it to work in the morning. If you wouldn't mind closing the door gently as you go out. Other people do live in the block, as it happens.'

After a pause she added, 'Goodbye. Best of luck at the next concert. Candidly, you'll need it.'

She vanished into the kitchen.

Albert's feet came unstuck from the carpet. They took a pace or two, wavered, veered, carried him across the room. The kitchen, he discovered, was sizeable. The wall-tiling was marine blue. Jennifer was lowering crockery into the sink. Her back was turned to him. She was leaning over the stainless steel with a hand on one of the taps; beneath the skirt, the slim calves of her boots were together, straight and firm. Her neck and shoulders looked insubstantial by contrast. Like a child's.

That, too, was the way they felt. Under his fingers the flesh was soft and warm, squirming as it resisted. Albert was in no mood for resistance.

Choking sounds came from her. Remembering what she had said about others in the block, he tightened his grasp. She mustn't make a noise that would disturb them.

He had no set plan. First he wanted to hurt her, subdue her. Then . . . make her listen. He had a conviction that, throughout the evening, he had been failing to make contact with her, with the real Jenny. To do so now demanded a physical effort, and this at least was within his resources, if he applied himself. Arms were beating at him. He managed to pin them with his elbows while retaining his grip. Both of them were doubled over the sink. An undignified posture, but there was no one to see them and it would perhaps teach her a mighty lesson, fetch her off her pedestal, make her see things his way. The choking had stopped. That was good. She was starting to co-operate.

You're tedious, Mr Albert Hall.

She wouldn't be bored now. This was action. He gave her a shake or two, asserting himself. It was like handling a heavy feather bolster. He let her subside.

She sagged over the edge of the sink, both arms trailing. His elbows were no longer needed to keep them in check. Really, she had given up absurdly easily. As he had suspected, she was all bombast, no core. Her body was now completely relaxed. But he wasn't interested. Not any more. He had made his point.

She wouldn't look at him again with that cool smile of disdain. No, sir. He'd given her something to think about. And if he was no longer around when she felt like expressing her thoughts, she had no one to blame but herself. She had had her chance.

He took his hands away.

She hung on the sink, her hair spread over the crockery at its base.

Stepping back, he surveyed her critically.

She looked somewhat ridiculous.

'You can stand up now,' he said curtly. 'Your seeming docility fails to impress me.'

The phrase pleased him. It was worth repeating. He said it again, and a third time. She didn't react, but he wasn't fooled. She wasn't going to yield in a hurry, not she. It would take time. They had lots of that.

'I didn't want to be rough,' he explained to her curved

spine. 'You left me with no alternative.'

Returning to the living-room, he wandered over to the record-player and found that a disc was already in place. Switching on, he waited expectantly.

Mozart's 23rd Piano Concerto. He listened to a few bars before strolling back.

'Why don't you come out and talk?'

He went forward, touched her shoulder.

After that, quietly, he let himself out of the building.

CHAPTER 3

'There's only one thing for it,' I said. 'You'll have to go to the police.'

Albert shook his head. 'I can't do that.' His head went on shaking, as though my words had activated a small electric motor inside his neck muscles.

'You've no choice.'

'I'll get done for murder.'

'You'll get done anyway. Make things easier for yourself, Albo. Liaise with the law. It's the only course.'

I was talking, I hoped, rationally. Beneath my outward calm, however, I was shaken and appalled. It wasn't just the thing itself, although nothing remotely like it had fallen from a height to hit me before: it was the involvement of Albert, of all people in the world. From the shelter of my fairly conventional observations, I was fighting to adapt to new, undreamed-of conditions.

To gain a breathing space I laced Albert's coffee with brandy for the second time, then poured myself a substantial measure and returned to my seat to nurse it with an appearance of dispassionate reflection.

Albert muttered something under his breath. I said, 'What?'

'They'd never believe it was an accident.'

'You could give them the chance.'

He slopped coffee into the saucer. 'I've swilled enough of this tonight,' he said with a kind of groan, 'to last me six months.' He lowered the cup and saucer to the floor. 'Why,' he asked, 'should I give them the chance? We both know how they'll react.'

I gestured. 'I don't think we ought to assume anything. From what you've told me, you could make out a pretty good case of provocation. You were simply reacting to a blatant—'

'Inside her own home?' he said sharply. 'Don't talk rot.'

'You could say she invited you back, then turned nasty . . . threatened you with blackmail or something. Who's to prove otherwise? You told her to keep her accusations to herself, one thing led to another, there was a row, a struggle developed . . .'

'You're overlooking one thing,' he interrupted. 'I'm not telling any story like that, because I'm not going to the police. I'm not getting myself involved.'

Studying him at that moment, I noted for some reason how the middle area of his rather wiry, grey-flecked hair had been steered forward in subtle parabolas to mask the incipient baldness of his temples. They were high, surprised temples. In shock, as he was now, his eyes seemed to be an inch or two above nose level. I felt an insane urge to lean forward, drag them down with my thumbs.

'Whether you like it or not,' I said, 'you are involved.'

'It doesn't follow.'

I spoke gently. 'Albo, you're not thinking straight. A dozen people at least will remember seeing you and Jennifer together at the concert. Half a dozen more at the coffee-bar later. Others on the Tube. Quite possibly, neighbours saw you arrive at her place. They do, you know. You think windows are curtained, when in fact—'

'That's all quite irrelevant.' Stretching across to my

glass-topped square table, he extracted a cigarette from my private supply in its rosewood container and replanted it between his quivering lips. Then he scrabbled a flame from my table lighter and in a bungling, hit or miss fashion created smoke which commenced to pour from both of his nostrils like the emissions of a dragon in some animated Disney cartoon. I watched spellbound. Never before had I seen him a prey to tobacco. 'They may have noticed her,' he resumed, coughing stealthily, 'in the company of a man. Can they name him? Identify him?'

'They might well describe him. Then, with the traces you'll have left behind in the flat . . .'

'Traces?'

'There's always something,' I said angrily. 'You're sure to have left all kinds of incriminating evidence. Fingerprints. Any amount of things.'

Slowly his head got into a shaking rhythm again. 'I don't think so.'

'How can you possibly be certain?'

'I can't,' he conceded, his lips working overtime on the filter tip. 'Not without taking a second look.'

'You'd better pop back, then,' I said sardonically.

'That's just what I think.'

My stare became fixed. 'You can't be serious?'

'Never more so.'

Leaping up, he toured the room in a series of nervy surges, chewing at the cigarette rather than smoking it, knocking furniture with his bony knees and elbows. Without a doubt, Albert at his best was not an example of co-ordinated man: at rock bottom, he was a splay-limbed mess. 'The thing to understand, Steve,' he told his haggard reflection in my brass-framed mirror, 'is that I've got to get back there tonight—at once. I've got to make sure everything's watertight.'

I rose too, leaving my brandy where it was. 'You're going to try covering your tracks? You intend just to let her be found, and hope never to be linked with the incident? You're out of your mind.'

'I was,' he assented swiftly. 'At the time I came away I was half crazy . . . you're right. Now that I've had time to think, talk it over with you, I can see it's the only thing to do.'

'Talk it over? You've talked, I've listened. This is your lunatic solution, not mine. Count me out of it.'

He turned pleadingly. 'I'm appealing to you, Steve, as a partner and an old buddy. Help me out, will you?'

I spoke as rationally as I could. 'Just by staying silent, I'll be helping as much as anyone has a right to expect. Already you've made me an accessory to murder—you realize that?'

His reply staggered me. 'In that case, you might as well go one step further and do something practical. What's the difference?'

On the edge of an outburst, I checked myself. Albert was not himself. To say this of the average person would imply some degree of disturbance: in the case of my partner, I was beginning to suspect that it expressed no more than the literal truth. Somehow, Albert during the course of the evening had contrived to jump right out of character and land with both flat feet in disaster. Ordinary remonstrance wouldn't do. Deviousness was needed.

I moderated my tone. 'The difference is, we'll have to look at things pretty carefully before dashing back into trouble. That's all. The idea, I assume, is that I should drive you?'

He nodded eagerly. 'There's the time factor, you see. It's nearly three already.'

'I'm only too aware of that.'

'Besides, I've no other way of getting there. My own car's God knows where by now.' He slid me a glance. 'If you'd rather, I could borrow yours and drive myself.'

'No, thanks.' I didn't want him leaving my car at the

kerbside to be identified by all and sundry. 'If we're going, I'll take you and drop you off. I still think it's a barmy idea. How will you get back inside the apartment, for a start?'

He paused in the act of buttoning his coat. 'I don't think the door catch fastened as I let myself out. In fact, I'm certain of it. I was so intent on not making a sound . . .'

'Terrific,' I said. 'The lousy door's probably swung wide open by now. Beckoning to a passing patrol car.'

Again the head-shaking. 'It stuck in the frame, I remember. That's why it didn't lock. I was afraid to tug too hard in case it slammed. But it was reasonably tight, I'm positive.'

Picking up my car keys, I turned slowly back to him. 'One thing puzzles me, Albo.'

'What?' he said limply, pulling on his left glove.

'Why leave it this long? If you'd already decided to go back . . .'

'I hadn't. Not when you picked me up. My mind was in a whirl. Now I've had time to recover a bit, I can see what needs to be done.'

'So can I.'

'Just the same, Steve,' he said with a certain politeness, 'you'll go along with me, won't you?'

'I'm not at all sure about that.'

'I hope you are.' Still polite. 'After all, I'm not the only one who'd sooner avoid the attentions of the law, am I?'

Driving through the bleak streets back towards Finchley, I thought over the years I had known Albert.

Although we hadn't been at school together, we had attended neighbouring schools at the same time and had clashed at soccer matches. In a gangling, incohesive sort of way, Albert had played an intimidating game which had given him some status in my eyes, and a patchy friendship had developed.

It had not taken me long to discover the flaws in his make-up. Mine, doubtless, had just as speedily made themselves evident to him. Notwithstanding, our relationship had persisted after we left school. A factor in this, on my side, was Albert's possession of a pretty sister. Clare was violet-eyed, gigglesome, pliable and willing, and for a full fifteen months I was able to regard Albert with comparative equanimity as a potential brother-in-law, until the day that I met Veronica and was obliged to . . . But that, as I have always itched to write, is another story. Quite a number of stories, actually. Poor Clare. She married a stockbroker, eventually, and they live in Surrey with two daughters and six Jack Russells and a pony; and I hope she is exceedingly happy but I have the severest doubts.

In Albert's case, he kept up with me because, I like to think, he recognized in me the drive, the strength of purpose that he manifestly lacked. Albert could be obstinate, usually over trivialities: in major matters he dithered. He needed constant reassurance, perpetual shoring up. As a brother-in-law elect, I had done my best to provide the necessary materials, but after breaking with Clare I lost touch, not surprisingly, with her family as well, and for four years Albert passed out of my life.

Only to reappear when I least expected him. It was at a reception in a marquee on the site of a project by Huntley Homes, a Reading-based development company with which I was then associated. Somebody announced that a representative of a firm of timber-frame suppliers wished to have a word with me, and when he was steered over I was startled to find myself in the saturnine presence of Albert, whose delight at our reunion was disproportionate but flattering. After the reception I took him to dinner. He was, he revealed, contemplating a move.

'Timber trade's all very fine, Steve, but it's hardly the career I had in mind to carve out.' Albert-like, he was totally unconscious of the *mot*. 'To be honest, I'm more interested in property.'

'Who isn't?' I eyed him across the plates. 'I might be leaving Huntley's myself, fairly soon,' I told him.

'Quitting the business?'

'Far from it. Starting up on my own. I reckon I know enough by now to make a go of it.'

I remember eyeing him again. From the other side of the table he was attending earnestly to my words, the follower waiting to be led. It was this that decided me. 'I'll probably be needing some help,' I added casually. 'You wouldn't be interested, I suppose?'

From there, events were rapid. Within three months, Newstyle Properties had become a reality, with myself at the helm and Albert hovering and twittering as first mate, a demon for work, malleable, anxious to please. The more I write about Albert, the more he seems to emerge as a creature of my own convenience, an object of derision: if this is the impression I have given, I should like to dilute it a little. In some ways, I had respect for the man. He was loyal. He knew his job. He had a knack of knowing where to go for the materials we needed for the apartment conversions we were undertaking, at keen prices, in various parts of the Home Counties. In this and certain other ways, he was invaluable. He also had something of an eye for likely properties, plus an instinct for guessing the minimum acceptable offer required in most cases. He had many virtues. Had it been otherwise, I should not have made him my partner.

I was reflecting on this when he stirred in his seat, began peering through the side windows, twisting to stare at the road behind. I said, 'What's up?'

'Can't quite see where we are . . .'

'Just coming up to the call box where you rang me from. You said you could find your way from there.'

'I don't know.' He sounded dubious. 'I've no recollection of this street at all. Which way did I come from?'

'How the hell should I know? You just appeared.'

He scratched his scalp underneath the fur hat. I recognized the mannerism. More than with most people, it denoted an intense anguish, a freezing of Albert's mental processes as a consequence of fright and desperation. I had witnessed it before. 'I can't remember,' he repeated tremulously. 'I've no idea which way I took from her place.'

'All right. Don't flap. Which Tube station did you travel to on the way there?'

He looked at me blankly. 'I didn't notice.'

'For Pete's sake . . . Was it Finchley Central?'

'Honestly, Steve, I haven't a clue. I was too busy following the girl.'

I stopped the car at a T-junction. 'How far did you follow her on foot?'

'A fair way. Several streets.'

'Catch sight of any names?'

His pupils went opaque. Finally, with a hideous inevitability, his head started to shake. 'I was concentrating on staying in touch with her. You know how it is, when you're trying to keep someone in view . . .'

'I don't, but I suppose I can imagine.' I regarded him stonily. 'You're not well acquainted with this part of London?'

'It's off my patch.'

'For your information, there's East Finchley Tube station, then Finchley Central, followed by West Finchley. Somehow I don't think we've time for an experimental sortie out of each before daybreak.'

He looked around huntedly. 'Back up to the call box again. We'll have to start from there.'

'If you really want to pursue this insane—'

'It's not a question of wanting,' he said, in the monotone of despair.

With a deep, deep sigh I reversed the car fifty yards to the point abreast of the call box where I had parked before. If a patrol car crew happened to be observing, I thought, we were fair game for detention on suspicion. The street was a dreary specimen of North London nocturnal abandonment: a tired amalgam of apartment blocks, occasional shopfronts, the odd bank. The lighting was fiercely white, interspersed with pools of black dejection. Applying the handbrake with an irritable heave, I switched off the engine and contemplated the prospect.

'Shoe leather from here, then?'

Without answering, Albert opened his door and struggled out. With a hand on the bonnet, he stared for a few seconds at the T-junction before switching his attention to a nearby side road on our left. I climbed out to join him. He flicked his head.

'I think I may have come along there.'

'So let's try it.' Locking the steering and doors, I gave the car a metaphorical rallying pat and breathed a short prayer over it, then jostled Albert, none too gently, into motion. 'If you see anything that looks familiar, bawl out. I'll try to keep general track of our bearings. If you're pretty sure it's wrong after we've gone a few hundred yards, say so and we'll turn back, try another way.'

As we set off, his uncertainty was obvious. Clearly, he had paid not the slightest attention to his whereabouts either before or after the catastrophe, and although I could understand the reasons for his negligence I was furious with him. Setting a smart pace, I said morosely, 'I suppose it's no use asking you to estimate the time you'd been walking, or how fast, before you reached the call box.'

'What time did I phone you?'

'One fifteen, almost to the minute.'

'I left her place at twelve fifty-five,' he said promptly, to my amazement. 'As I was closing the inner door, I spotted her clock on the end wall. Five to one, it said. I recall that distinctly.'

'It might have been wrong.'

'Doubt it,' he said through chattering teeth. 'It was electric. Normally they're dead right.'

'Okay. We'll assume it was. Twenty minutes. When you came away, did you walk or run?'

'Walked. Quite slowly. I didn't want to attract attention.'

'You couldn't have covered a great distance. Seen anything yet that grabs you?'

His head wagged. Continuing to a bend in the road, we halted to survey the next ill-lit vista. The head-wagging gained emphasis. 'I'm sure this wasn't it,' he said.

Wordlessly I turned him about, marched him back. Once more in the call box region, I spun a mental coin and propelled him away to the right, in the opposite direction from that in which I had arrived on both occasions. My reasoning was that, if he had seen nothing from the car that jogged his memory, the odds were slightly in favour of his having approached from the north. At the T-junction we turned left and then, at my instigation, right again. This street was almost entirely residential, a crescent of Edwardian-looking four-storey houses with huge bay windows and semi-basements, and area railings held in place by crumbling stone pillars. Albert began to sniff the air.

'This looks more promising.'

'Plenty of other London streets like it,' I cautioned him.

Completing the curve to the far end, we forked right again, descending a sharp gradient that led past a gigantic gloomy church into a narrower street where the houses were terraced, butting directly on to the pavements. Excitement gripped Albert.

'I passed that church!'

'How long had you been walking?'

'Five, ten minutes. I can't say exactly.'

At a multiple crossroads he became flummoxed. A heavy goods vehicle thundered past us from west to east, and the cacophony of its progress seemed to disorientate him, fracture the image that had shown signs of forming in his mind. He wandered eastwards for a short distance, hesitated, returned to the intersection, headed north. My watch said nearly four o'clock. I caught up with him.

'Have you any idea, or are you just drifting?'

'I'm fairly sure we're on the right track,' he said, on the note of obstinacy that was an infallible contradiction of the utterance.

'If we ever do find the place,' I argued, 'it's odds on we'll be spotted trying to get in. Some insomniac is sure to be at a window, sipping weak tea. Wouldn't it be safer to leave things as they are? You said yourself you didn't think you'd left any traces.'

Making no reply, he quickened his strides. I put a restraining hand on the rodlike flesh inside his sagging coat-sleeve. 'Albert,' I said. 'Stop a minute.'

Reluctantly he turned to face me. Keeping my hold of him, I spoke softly but plainly. 'Suppose I were to turn now and make for the nearest police station, tell them just what you've told me . . . what would you do?'

The look he fixed upon me defied diagnosis. After a brief interval he said, 'Go ahead, then, why don't you? Find a panda car, report the occurrence.'

'It was just a hypothesis.'

'I know it was.' He nodded past me at the illuminated window of a newsagent's on the other side of the street. 'I seem to remember that. It's not far from here.'

I let him go ahead. I wasn't sure whether he was trying to cover his indecisiveness or genuinely felt that he was homing in. There was an element of bluster in his apparent purposefulness. For my part, I was tired, cold and dispirited. What in hell, I thought, were we doing, the pair of us, trudging London streets at four in the morning in quest of a fantasy? I was starting to feel convinced that Albert had imagined it all. If he had ever shown symptoms of possessing an imagination, I should have been confident from the outset.

'Along here,' he said in low-voiced exultancy.

'How do you know?'

'These were the buildings. They're an odd lot, mostly flat conversions, and I remember noticing one or two were up for sale. There ought to be a sign . . . That's it. There.'

He pointed to a sale board fastened to a front window of one of the properties. As he had said, the structures were of a weirdly indefinite design, mostly two and three storeys, belonging to no identifiable period and having no uniformity of theme: it looked like a street of elderly cottages that had been bludgeoned into pint-sized apartments by a variety of insensitive hands. Behind the façades, I guessed, were doors leading off at angles, floors at different levels, a general muddle of domestic topography. All at once, it was easier to credit Albert's description of an L-shaped room split by a couple of steps. He was sniffing along like a beagle scenting a rabbit. 'Five or six doors on,' he muttered hoarsely, stabbing me on with a thumb. 'I caught up with her just as she was . . . This is it. I'm positive.'

He stopped opposite a door with a slim glazed strip running down the centre and the numerals '31' in chrome screwed to the lintel. At his elbow, I glanced swiftly both ways along the street before gesturing him into action. Stepping forward, he inclined himself lightly against the woodwork.

For a second or two he stayed there, as though adhesion had occurred. Again I flapped at him. Bracing a foot at an angle, he gave the door a nudge. With a faintly sucking rasp it released itself from the frame and swung inwards, hitting something and coming to rest. Albert turned to look at me.

My gesture this time had a hint of wildness. Obedient to its message, he went through the opening and stood aside while I followed. Between us we pushed the door carefully back into place and were in darkness.

His breath hissed into my ear. 'Straight ahead. I'll close the inner door before we put lights on.'

The living-room was, indeed, as he had sketched it for me. The first thing I noticed was the electric wall-clock, announcing that it was eight minutes past four. It tallied precisely with my watch, which I had set by the late news bulletin. Like a non-swimmer testing the ice on a pond, Albert moved forward, tugging mechanically at his glove-fingers.

I said sharply, 'Keep your gloves on.'

Hastily he thrust his fingers back. In the artificial light his face was ashen. Now that we were here, ninety per cent paralysis seemed to have overtaken him. Stepping past, I paused at a door on our right.

'Kitchen?'

He gave a single nod. It was more like a twitch. I drew breath. I knew I wouldn't like what I was going to see. I knew Albert would like it even less. What I didn't know was exactly how either of us would be affected. There were no precedents to guide me. Property development was our scene, not violent crime. My fingers froze momentarily on the door handle.

'Don't open it,' Albert implored suddenly.

In a reflex spasm my hand went down, freeing the catch.

The blackness of the kitchen was only faintly alleviated by the glow from the living-room wall-lamps. The outline of a worktop was just visible. I fumbled for a switch. Somewhere behind me, Albert was breathing heavily.

There was no switch, but my fingers brushed a pull-cord, trapping it at the third attempt. A tug induced light from a somewhat low-wattage bulb attached to the ceiling. I took two paces inside.

Almost immediately I retreated to the living-room. Albert was immobile against a wall, an arm across his eyes and forehead. I touched his shoulder.

'You say you left her with head and shoulders in the sink, wedged under the taps?'

Lowering his arm, he gazed at me dully. 'I didn't try to shift her. Is she still there?'

'There's a body,' I said, sweating, 'in exactly that position. Only it doesn't look like a girl's. It's wearing trousers.'

CHAPTER 4

The bed in my spare room was unmade. When I returned to it with blankets, however, Albert was lying fully clad on the mattress in an attitude of total exhaustion, open-eyed but seemingly unaware of his surroundings. Dropping a blanket or two over the lower half of him, I doused the light and left the room, leaving the door ajar.

After washing the brandy glass and coffee cup, and cleaning the ashtray, I sank into an armchair with my legs outflung and balanced the heel of one shoe on the toe of the other.

I tried to do some thinking.

My brain is of the functional variety. Given a set of factors, each one relevant to the remainder, it can normally come up with a conclusion satisfactory to all parties and beneficial to at least one—usually myself. It does, however, have its limitations. Deprived of substance to bite on, it tends to go into a baffled decline.

I could feel it happening now. And I knew I mustn't allow the condition to worsen. A quick decision was vital.

Albert had been less than no help. His state on the return trip had bordered on the cataleptic, and although, once back in my apartment, he had found his tongue to the extent of replying to some of my questions, they had clouded rather than cleared the picture. I was left with a sensation of trying to swim through chilled treacle to an unknown destination on the far side of a foggy lake.

A fresh approach was demanded. Reaching for a notepad and ballpen, I jotted down the gist of our exchange.

MYSELF: Are you perfectly certain you attended a concert last night at the Royal Albert Hall? Do you have a ticket stub?

ALBERT: No. I think I stuffed it down the side of the seat. But I know I was there. I remember booking a week ago.

M: Can you recall striking up a conversation with anyone else, apart from Jennifer?

A: I said good-evening to the chap on the door.

M: The man we saw in Jennifer's kitchen . . . did you recognize anything about him?

A: How the hell would I know? His face was hidden.

M: What about his clothing?

A: I only saw him for a second.

M: We should have lifted him out of the sink. If I'd had my wits about me, I'd never have let you rush me off like that. We were bloody idiots to panic.

A: He looked just like she did.

M: You mean the position he was in? Listen, Albert. When you left her place the first time, could she have been shamming dead?

A: I can't say. It's possible, I suppose. I was in a daze. Couldn't take it in.

M: Alternatively, she might simply have been unconscious? One way or another, she either left the kitchen after you'd gone or she was taken out and put somewhere else. If she left under her own steam, where did she go?

A: To get help, maybe. From a neighbour.

M: Who then proceeded to get killed himself, and dumped over the sink in her place?

A: Which would mean somebody else is involved.

M: Unless Jennifer herself was trying to set you up. But that's ridiculous. She couldn't have known she was going to meet you. She couldn't have counted on your behaving in the way you did. All the initiative came from you.

A: The entire thing's crazy.

M: Pointless, anyhow. It doesn't achieve anything. If there were signs of an attempted robbery . . .

A: Steve, I must lie down.

M: I'll make up a bed. What about Mel?

A: She won't have missed me.

M: Still, I'd better give her a call. After all, she is your wife.

Leaving the armchair, I crossed the room quietly and pushed open the spare bedroom door.

Albert was motionless under the blankets, his head turned to one side on the pillow. Breath snorted in and out of his open mouth. The sleeping tablets I had given him had evidently asserted themselves. Closing the door softly, I went over to my desk in the alcove and picked up the phone.

The ringing tone bleated for a long time before the receiver at the far end was lifted.

'Yes . . . h'llo?'

The voice was choked with sleep. I said, 'Mel, it's Steve. I know it's six in the morning, but this is just to let you know that Albo's here, at my place.'

'What's he doing there?'

'I won't try to explain now, but he's had a bit of a night. He's . . . sleeping it off in my spare bed.'

'Silly faggot,' she said indifferently. 'What made you think I might be worried?'

'Just thought you should know.'

'Thanks,' she said, and hung up.

Cradling the receiver, I stood looking pensively at the Stubbs original on the wall at the back of the alcove.

In her own way, I thought, Mel was right. Silliness was precisely what Albert suffered from.

Any other man would have made a show, at least, of fighting to save his marriage. It wasn't as though he didn't care. He cared enough to go to elaborate lengths to make it appear that he didn't. In a front-line soldier such an affectation of regardlessness might have been admirable; in a husband . . . He really had asked for what he was getting.

Mel was hardly the sort of girl—if such a sort exists—to be taken for granted. Certainly not by the Alberts of this world. Eight months after their marriage, to my knowledge, she had launched her search for consolation, and it hadn't taken her long to find it. It had taken Albert perhaps slightly longer to discover that he had lost his rights to her, and considerably longer to develop his counter-measures, which amounted in effect to doing nothing. No peace moves, no supplication on his part. His stubborn streak took over. Mel would return to him on his terms, or not at all.

This was how I had gauged his response, and nothing that had since occurred or failed to occur had contradicted the assessment. Abandoned in the wilderness, Albert had gone blundering in pursuit of alternative happiness, while Mel competently looked after her own. Time, he seemed to imagine, was on his side. She would drift back in the end. I could have disabused him, but our partnership was a working one, not an emotional therapy clinic.

Going out to the lobby, I felt through the pockets of his coat and jacket. There was no ticket. But in the breast pocket of the jacket I found a leaflet containing a list of concert dates at the Royal Albert Hall, with the previous evening's programme heavily ringed in purple ink. Not that this proved anything, but it added weight to Albert's insistence that he had been there to hear it. I could check further at the office.

Dousing the living-room lights, I went through to my own bedroom, took off my shoes and lay on the bed.

At eight-thirty I looked in on Albert.

He was lying on his left side, still as death. Moving round the bed, I ascertained that he was breathing. He was a fairly good colour. I went to the kitchen and made tea.

By soon after nine I had got him to the breakfast table and forcibly fed him half a slice of wheaten toast garnished with honey. In the meantime I had telephoned the office and told Amanda—early at her station as usual—that we would both be in rather late. In addition, the papers had arrived.

There was a great deal about the economic situation. There was nothing at all about a corpse in a kitchen.

Fleet Street, I reminded myself, stopped printing before dawn.

The radio news, however, was likewise devoid of sensation. The nine o'clock bulletin was full of a peace feeler put out by the Prime Minister to the Unions: 'A gleam of hope,' burbled the newscaster, 'on a darkening industrial scene.' A kidnap victim had been found alive and well beside a highway in Northern Italy. No one had been found slumped over a kitchen sink in North London.

As we pulled on our coats I said, 'Hadn't you better

make some enquiries about your car?'
Albert returned from afar. 'Who do I contact?'
'Try the police at Hyde Park.'
Terror seized his features. I added patiently, 'They can't link you with anything. You're just a motorist, calling to ask which pound your car was towed away to for the night.'
'What if I was seen leaving it with Jennifer?'
I looked at him for a moment. 'The point is, you weren't seen leaving it with a man.'
He caught his breath.
'Or were you?' I asked.
His body stiffened. 'I wasn't suffering from delusions last night, Steve. How could I have made all that up about her?'
'I'm not saying you did. I'm merely suggesting there could be things you've forgotten.'
'In other words, if I'm not deluded I'm amnesiac, and if I can't—'
'This isn't getting us far,' I observed. 'Call the cops and get it over with.'
'What's the number?'
I found it for him. While he was dialling I went to the window to study the morning. It was dull but dry. Half a mile away, the dome of St Paul's stood massively against a metallic sky. As a place in which to live, this area of the capital appealed to me. After business hours, when the City traffic had drained away to the suburbs, the district was quieter than the average rural village, and much as I like a bit of life I prefer to go in quest of it in my own time and style, not have it crowding my door. At this hour of the morning, of course, the streets were frantic. Five floors down, vehicles and people were interweaving like twill, their racket reduced to a dull rumble by the double glazing.
Doug, the stoical Cockney who manned his news-stand

five days a week in front of the travel agency building opposite, had company this morning, I noticed. Leaning against the wooden side of Doug's kiosk stood a burly youngish man wearing a bright blue padded jacket zipped up to his neck and a circular yellow woollen hat pulled down to his ears. Arms folded, he was gazing skywards along the street as though awaiting the promise of spring. He had no tools, but I guessed he was waiting to be picked up by a council truck.

Behind me, Albert said, 'Hullo. I wonder if you can help me. I had to leave my car at Marble Arch last night—a bit of an emergency—and I expect you had to tow it away. Could you tell me . . .'

He paused to listen. Presently he said, 'Oh, I see. That's fine, then. I can pick it up at once? How much . . . ? I see. I'll be along in an hour or so. Many thanks. 'Bye now.'

'Problem solved?' I asked.

'It's in a pound off the Bayswater Road,' he replied absently, hanging up.

'No hassle?'

'They were quite pleasant about it.'

'Routine to them. And one plus factor is, it confirms what you were saying, to some extent.'

'About what?'

'Not having delusions last night.'

'I told you I didn't.'

As we plummeted in the lift to the basement garage, I said, 'Shall I drive you over to fetch your car?'

'No, don't bother. I'll get the Tube from Victoria. One of us had better show up at the office in good time.'

Albert had the fixed notion that the absence of either of us for longer than an hour or two at a stretch meant a week's disruption of our business affairs. Privately, I considered that Amanda and Bob Callis, our site surveyor and factotum, could cope between them with anything that was likely to arise; but I allowed Albert to go on believing that he was indispensable. It was useful at times, and it kept him happy.

Driving out of the ramp into the street, I gave Doug's kiosk a glance before accelerating away. The man in the blue jacket was still propped against the boards. As we passed, he turned his head and logged our progress with a kind of detached intensity. I started to say, 'That guy over there . . .'

Then I had second thoughts, and stopped.

Albert gave no sign of having noticed. He seemed lost in a world of his own, and there he stayed all the way to Victoria Street. I made no move to break in for a rescue attempt. For the time being we had chewed things over enough. Let him retrieve his car, I thought, and return to the familiar environment of the office, where he could divert himself with a little work while awaiting the first editions of the evening papers. Depending on what we read or failed to read in their columns, we could plot our next move, should one seem necessary. I could see no alternative to playing things by ear.

Dropping him as near to the Tube station as I could, I said calmingly, 'Take your time, old chap. No need to blow a gasket.' Stiff-legged, he walked across the road to the subway. I watched him until the honking of an impeded cab-driver drove me away from the kerb. At that moment I felt sorrier for Albert than I had in all the previous years of our acquaintance. The figure he cut had always struck me as essentially ridiculous. The element of pathos had escaped me before.

As I entered the outer office, Amanda looked up brightly. 'No panics, Mr Cassell. Maurice Foreman telephoned, but he said it wasn't urgent. The mail's on your desk.'

'Thanks, Amanda. What's that you're pounding out, a dossier for MI5?'

She smiled dutifully. 'Correspondence for Mr Hall,' she

said on a note of faint reproof. 'He left some for me.'

'No kidding?'

Albert's correspondence had come to acquire the status of a myth and a legend. If a way existed to take twenty paragraphs to explain what could have been summarized in two, Albert discovered it. He wrote letters to people who could have been telephoned, and he composed schedules for despatch to people who would have been content with a postcard. He was a joyful slave to the dictaphone. Amanda, a creature of placid disposition, humoured him most of the time, rebelling only on selected occasions, and then with deference. I left her flicking at the keyboard and went through to the main office, subdivided by wood and glass to give each of us—Bob, Albert and myself—some essential privacy without placing us in worlds apart. Bob, I could see at a glance, was out somewhere. Envelopes and a packet or two littered my desktop. Sweeping them aside, I dumped my briefcase and touched the intercom switch.

'Amanda, what time do the evening papers get on the streets, do you know?'

'Soon after ten, I should think. They're probably on sale now.'

'Would you be very kind and get one of each for me?'

'Yes, of course.' A welcome break for her, I thought, tackling the mail.

After I had slit all the envelopes I was faced with a mound of letters and documents that I couldn't bring myself to scan. Thrusting them aside again, I returned to the outer office. Amanda had gone for the papers. A partly finished letter sat in her machine. I stooped to inspect it. The addressees were Messrs Freecroft and Abbott, Home Accessories Suppliers, of Basingstoke, and the burden of Albert's convoluted message appeared to be that unless they could guarantee delivery within two weeks of chrome door-handles and window-stays in the quantities applied for, Newstyle Properties would feel justified in terminating their existing contract and taking their custom elsewhere. It was, for Albert, an uncommonly direct statement of intent. In this instance, evidently, the iron had entered his soul. Tapping the sheet approvingly with a finger, I turned as Amanda reappeared with the newspapers and a copy of *World Citizen*, which she placed carefully on a shelf alongside her desk. She saw me throw it a glance.

'Lunchtime reading,' she remarked, 'for the liberated female. Really I should be mugging up my first-aid literature. I've a practical exam at evening class tonight. Here are your papers, Mr Cassell. Shocking murder in North London—read all about it! Mr Cassell? Mr *Cassell*? Coo-ee! Are you feeling all right?'

I must have given a lurch. Grabbing the desk edge, I steered a grin in her general direction. 'Came out on an empty stomach. Didn't sleep too well.'

'You do look a bit washed out.' Sympathy expressed itself in the momentary droop of her rather wide, full-lipped mouth. 'How about some coffee?'

'I think you're on my side, Amanda.'

The mouth widened again. 'It's only because I need some myself. Soon I've got to start reading about intravenous injections. I'll need all my fortitude for that.'

Contriving some meaningless rejoinder, I planted money for the papers in her in-tray, took them through to my own desk, spread them out. My lungs and stomach felt as if they had fused together. At first none of the headlines seemed to make any sense: I took in the words but the message remained right outside in the dark. Presently, however, getting my respiratory system under control a little, I began to scan them more comprehendingly.

There was nothing on either front page about a North London killing. Could Amanda, making an idle joke, have hit by chance upon the one form of words calculated to knock me sideways? Wildly I reversed one of the papers, exposing the back page.

And there it was, in bold type at the foot of a column: 'Coloured Youth Stabbed in Pub Brawl'. It had happened in Islington.

Collapsing slowly into my chair, I read the sketchy details, making sure. Then I hunted back through both editions. There was no other story relating to dead bodies.

Leaning back, I breathed massively five times, drummed my fingers.

Albert, I thought, should be back in half an hour. No doubt bringing his own copies of the first editions. Later in the day we should both be sending out casually for more. Albert would suggest, and I should assent to, a bar lunch at Muldoon's, where the TV was invariably tuned to the midday newscast. Meanwhile, concentration was going to be tricky.

Retrieving some of the mail, I glanced through it again, made a note or two, strove in vain to decipher the motivation behind a seemingly harmless communication from a solicitor acting for someone who had purchased a Newstyle conversion in Cheam and was a little concerned about damp. Albert's province, I decided, leaving the letter on his desk. He would be back shortly.

In the adjoining office, Amanda's machine chattered softly, with barely a pause, for an hour.

At noon, I went through and asked whether she had heard anything from Mr Hall.

'No, Mr Cassell. He hasn't rung in. Were you expecting him to?'

'No, I was expecting him to arrive in person. He must have been delayed.'

'Where was he going this morning?' She reached for the office diary.

'Only to pick up . . .' I hesitated. 'He had to collect his car,' I said vaguely. 'It shouldn't have taken him long.'

'Perhaps he drove on somewhere afterwards. To look at a property or something.' She shook her head over the diary page. 'He wasn't scheduled for anything. But he might have acted on impulse.'

'He'd have let me know.'

'Shall I try his home?' she suggested, extending a hand to the switchboard.

'No, don't do that. Well, all right . . . get the number for me, will you, and I'll have a word with Mrs Hall. If she's there. He may have been in touch with her.'

Amanda's face remained expressionless. She was no fool, but equally she was a well-schooled, disciplined office secretary with all the qualities of discretion that went with the job, and without a lead from me she was not going out on a limb. And I wasn't proposing to give any sort of a lead. Returning to the main office, I waited for the phone to bleat.

Absurdly, I jumped when it did so. It occurred to me then that there had been no incoming calls whatever during the two hours since I had arrived. A remarkable hiatus. I couldn't remember a comparable one.

I lifted the instrument. 'Mel? Apologies for disturbing you again. I just wondered whether Albo had been in contact with you, by any chance.'

'Since when?'

'This morning.'

'I thought he was with you.'

'He was, till about ten. Then he went off to reclaim his car—it was towed away last night. He hasn't shown up again yet.'

'Maybe they've towed him away as well.'

'You've not heard from him, then?'

'Try to guess.'

'Well, I just thought I'd ask. He may have travelled

straight on to one of the sites without letting me know, though it's not like him.'

'You said earlier he'd made a night of it. Perhaps he's been taken ill in a toilet.'

She sounded fully as concerned as a blood sportsman speculating upon the likely fate of the umpteenth pheasant in the heather. I wondered whether Amanda was plugged in. 'He seemed pretty fit in himself when I dropped him off. Possibly he thought he'd mentioned something to me, but hadn't.'

'He'll turn up in due course,' she said coolly.

'Oh sure. If he does come home first, get him to call me, will you?'

'If I see him.'

I waited, but she said nothing more, so I hung up.

With suspiciously good timing, Amanda opened the door and showed me her head and a shoulder. 'When would you like me to go for lunch, Mr Cassell?'

'It rather depends. Is Bob going to be back soon?'

'Doubt it. He had to go out to Greenwich.'

'Would now suit you?'

'Fine.' She gave me a flash of white teeth.

'Unless Mr Hall returns first, I'll wait until you get back before I go myself.'

'Okay,' she said cheerfully. Closing the door, she thumped around for a minute or so, getting herself ready; eventually I heard the outer door open and close. Investigating, I confirmed that she had gone. Seating myself at the switchboard, I looked up the number of Hyde Park Police Station for the second time that morning, and dialled it.

To an answering voice I said, 'Perhaps you can help me. A friend of mine went along this morning to get his car back from one of your pounds. Can you tell me—'

'Hold on.' The line clicked several times.

Involuntarily, I cut the connection.

Quitting Amanda's chair, I paced to the window and glanced along the street. It presented the usual weekday picture: cars, vans, people. All of them intent upon their own affairs. A normal scene. The sky had cleared, and weak sunlight sprawled over the brickwork, although to judge from the antics of some vagrant newsprint in the gutter the wind had freshened. On the far side, nearly opposite our premises, somebody was standing with pocketed hands on the top step of the main entrance to an office block. The pockets belonged to a bright blue padded jacket, zipped to the neck. A circular yellow woollen hat was pulled down to the ears above it.

The eyes were looking towards me.

Stepping sharply backwards, I collided painfully with a chair. Massaging my shinbone, I hobbled to a position from which I could still see across the street without making myself obvious. From personal observation at other times, I knew it to be virtually impossible for an outsider's gaze to penetrate the grime of the office windows to the extent of distinguishing interior features: for all this, I felt exposed, like raw meat hung in a butcher's, ripe for fingering. The inspection from across the street was steadfast. People went past him, up and down the steps, in and out of the swing doors: he never moved.

Did I know him? Ransacking forgotten crevices of my memory, I knew that I didn't. Men who attired themselves in eiderdown and tea cosy and stood motionless on streets were beyond my circle of acquaintances, immediate or remote. For a minute or two I kept him in view, waiting for him to be joined by somebody, for a van to pull up at the kerbside, a group of ladder-hung colleagues to arrive. Before anything of the sort could occur, the switchboard behind me bleeped an incoming call.

With a sensation of faint thankfulness I lifted the receiver. From there, I was indisputably out of sight from the street. 'Newstyle Properties.'

'Mr Cassell?'

'Speaking.' A female voice, unidentifiable. Something about it, a guarded quality, made me obscurely uneasy on the instant. Images of ghosts past and present trooped across my mental skyline. 'How can I help you?' The overtones of this phrase, in my experience, tend to throw the other party on the defensive, particularly when uttered with soft courtesy in a lilting manner.

'I'm speaking,' said the voice, 'on behalf of Mr Hall.'

'Oh yes?' I said eagerly.

'You know Mr Hall, I believe.'

'He's my partner. Is anything wrong?'

'Something's very wrong, I'm afraid.'

I stared stupidly at the switchboard keys. The pause persisted. I said, 'Has there been an accident?'

'No. You could hardly call it that.'

'Who is this speaking?' I demanded.

'I'm speaking on behalf of Mr Hall.'

'Don't try to be clever with me. Who are you, and what's happened to my partner?'

'I hoped you might know.'

'I damn well don't. I'm expecting him here and he hasn't shown up—that's all I know. Now what the hell is your name? What connection do you have with Mr Hall and why do you want to—'

'He's often to be found at Finchley these days, isn't he?'

'What?'

'Finchley. North London. You must know that area.'

I said carefully, 'Parts of London I know. Other parts I'm less familiar with. It's the same with people. Some I know, a great many I don't. I'm afraid you come into the latter category. And unless you're willing to explain yourself, make it clear what you're calling about and what your interest is in the matter, I shall have no alternative but to—'

'You *have* no alternatives, Mr Cassell. None at all.'

'What's that supposed to mean?'

'As regards your partner, then: Mr Albert Hall. You can't be of any help?'

'I might be, if I knew what—'

'Very disappointing. But really only to be expected. I shall have to call back, then.'

I tried to unclench my teeth. 'If you can give me your name, I'll tell my partner you called.'

'No use, I'm afraid. It's not Mr Hall I shall be speaking to.'

'You've just said you'll call back.'

'Oh, you'll be hearing from me again. 'Bye, Mr Cassell.'

A loud buzzing came from the switchboard. The connection had been severed.

Slowly replacing the receiver, I stood looking down at it.

After a while I returned to the main office. Still littering my desk was the morning's mail, undealt with, undigested. One or two vital matters, I seemed hazily to recollect, had been included among the headed sheets that I had removed from their envelopes, scanned and pushed aside. I ought to re-examine them, establish priorities, give attention to the most urgent. Prompt action in all cases: the proud motto of the Newstyle operation. I had some free time. Why wasn't I making use of it?

Sitting on the desk edge, I stared at the nearest wall.

The voice had been strange to me. Of that I was in no doubt. It belonged to nobody with whom I had recently dealt, nor was it an echo from the past. It had been an ordinary, somewhat colourless feminine voice, devoid of any characteristic that might have set it apart from a dozen others, if one discounted the guarded note that had conveyed itself initially. After a sentence or two, that had seemed to disperse. From then on, each remark had been pitched on the same key, one of polite observation or enquiry, suggestive rather of regret than malevolence. And yet . . .

I ran the conversation back in my head. Viwed dispassionately, it had contained little of a contentious nature; on her part, at least. Any sparks that had flown were from my side. Had I reacted over-hastily?

There was, when you came to think about it, a fairly innocent construction to be placed upon virtually everything she had said. 'Something's very wrong, I'm afraid' . . . phrases like that were capable of perfectly harmless explanations. She might have been involved recently with Albert, lost touch with him through his fault or her own, yearned to pick up the threads. It didn't sound much like Albert, but now I could never be sure.

As for the reference to Finchley, that surely was coincidence. The district in question scarcely ranked as an obscure quarter of the capital. Which could account for her comment: 'You must know that area.' Another way of saying: 'You must have heard of it.' The kind of thing anyone might say. Even the phrase about having no alternatives was not, in itself, necessarily sinister, when you came to analyse it . . .

Pushing away from the desk, I walked to the partition and back.

There was nothing to be gained by trying to delude myself. The dialogue was still fresh in my mind, its cadences were clear; played back on whatever mental tape, the intelligence remained the same. Something about the call had been badly askew.

I wished Albert would walk in.

To feel this way was something of a novelty. Although our partnership was now into its sixth year and, by any normal business yardstick, could have been rated a rampant success, at no time in the course of those sixty-odd months had I felt any sense of dependence upon Albert's judgement. The fundamental Newstyle policies were my province, tacitly recognized as such. Albert was the latecomer who now contributed, so to speak, the legwork. He it was who had taken on the day-to-day supervision of our various projects, leaving me at liberty to tackle the longer-term planning.

The system had worked nicely. While valuing Albert's role, however, I had paused this side of adulation, never having questioned the real source of our prosperity. Now, suddenly, I found myself appraising the situation from a new slant.

The fact could not be blinked that, humdrum as Albert's daily activities might be, I had allowed myself to become almost wholly reliant upon them. Blot out Albert, and one was likely to witness the obliteration of a pyramid of interlocked parts, each relevant to the next, whose re-assembly would be a task of daunting magnitude.

In plain words, I couldn't do without the man.

The clump of the outer door ruptured my train of thought. Hopefully I went through to investigate. Amanda greeted me with her most blinding upper row of teeth.

'Sorry I'm a bit late, Mr Cassell. I was trying on shoes.'

'At least you're still around,' I said with mild sarcasm. 'Which is more than can be said for the residue of the staff. Bob's out at Greenwich, you say?'

'That's where he said he was going.'

'Any special reason?'

Her eyebrows shot up. 'To do with the Cedars conversion, I assume. Wasn't there some problem about door-frames?'

'Can he be got at?'

She glanced at the clock. 'He might be lunching in the Swan,' she said doubtfully.

'Be an angel and try.'

I hung at her shoulder while she dialled, waited, voiced

her request, waited. From where I stood, I heard the cry of a distant female voice: 'Is there a Mr Robert Callis in the bar?' Another wait. Amanda peeped up at me.

'If he's there, he won't take kindly to being . . . Hullo? Hi, Bob. Amanda. We tracked you down. Sorry to interrupt your meal. Mr Cassell would like a word.'

I took the receiver from her. 'Very sorry, Bob, to disturb you at lunch. Mr Hall isn't with you, by any chance?'

'No, I'm here by myself.' His diction was a little clogged. The Swan, I recalled, served succulent chicken in a basket.

'Seen him at all this morning?'

'Should I have done?'

'I only wondered if he'd paid an impulse visit to the site.'

'No reason for him to.' Bob sounded hurt. 'He sent me here to see to things.'

'I realize that. I just wanted to check that he hadn't driven out there for some other purpose.'

'If I do see him, is there a message?'

'Just ask him to contact me. Everything under control?'

'No problem. I'll be drifting on to Beckenham later this afternoon, all right? Apparently there's some hitch with sub-contractors. Unless you want me back in the office?'

'No. Do as you think best. 'Bye now.'

I handed the receiver back to Amanda. 'How many of the sites can we reach by phone?'

Her lips pursed, rather fetchingly. Something, I was never sure what, prevented our office treasure from qualifying as a sex bomb; but there were times when she came tantalizingly close. Drawing a desk file towards her, she began flicking through the cards.

'No chance at Epsom. Contractors haven't moved in. Croydon ditto. The rest should be possible. Depends who's around.' She glanced up again. 'Want me to . . . ?'

I patted her substantial shoulder. 'Sorry—but yes. It's rather important that I nail Mr Hall down to a location. He must be at one of the sites. There's nowhere else he's likely to have gone. Try 'em all, will you? Meanwhile I'll grab some lunch. If you do trace him, have him phone in urgently in about half an hour.'

'Don't bolt your food,' she said severely, starting to dial.

CHAPTER 5

The lunch bar at Muldoon's had a deserved reputation for fast service, but nobody had ever thought of calling it restful. If you went there you adapted to its pace and style, and to hell with contemplation.

Today the atmosphere suited me well. At this stage I didn't want to think too strenuously. Having placed an order for beef sandwiches with mustard and taken delivery of vodka and tonic, I looked round for a table but there was none to spare. The owner of a face I recognized signalled with a paw from the far end of the counter, so I jostled my way across.

'Pandemonium in here, as always,' he said, proffering a vacant stool. 'No Prince Consort today?'

'Albert's faded out on me,' I said, accepting the stool.

'Not quit?'

'Nothing so drastic. He's on site somewhere, incommunicado. Hence my harassed mien.'

'Come *on*, old boy. You're not telling us you miss him?'

What I should have liked to inform the pink, grinning countenance of Derek Spalding, whose sole claim upon my forbearance stemmed from his senior position within the Victoria Street branch of the clearing bank that housed the Newstyle Properties account, was that his conversational address not only lacked depth but was actively riddled with the disease of fatuity. It was not the first time I had experienced such an urge. Rarely before had I teetered so perilously on the brink. His bulging pupils, afire with inane fellowship, remained fastened upon mine in obvious expectation of a slyly malicious riposte. I decided to disappoint him.

'We do constitute a partnership, as it happens. Naturally there are times when I miss him.'

His face fell. That phrase can be overworked, but in this instance his features did actually drop, like those of a small boy told that he couldn't have a second helping. Salvaging gamely, he said, 'I dare say it can be useful to be in harness with someone like Albert. Pretty consistent, isn't he? Healthwise and attendance-wise and all that rot. *Dependable.* Genned-up, too, on the practical side, I imagine.' He seemed anxious to over-compensate for his earlier flippancy. 'Gives you a free hand to run the finances while he keeps tabs on the ops front.'

'I hope he feels it's a fair arrangement.'

Spalding tittered. 'No question of that. Shouldn't think he'd want to get involved in your fiscal juggling, you son of a tycoon.'

'I don't keep anything from him.'

'No more than you keep from the auditors, eh?' He slipped me a confidential nudge.

I said pleasantly, 'I've a nice, amicable understanding with Crabshaw's. They accept my little ways.'

'Meaning that other firms mightn't?'

'One tries not to be a slave to the rule-book. Enterprise can be terribly constricted that way.'

Spalding went through a pantomime of blocking an ear. 'Sorry? Didn't catch that.'

'Don't go getting the wrong idea, Derek.' I smiled at him, man to man, entrepreneur to backer. 'All I'm saying is, a spot of elasticity here and there—well, it does no harm, and it might often do a bit of good. This is what it's hard to explain to people like Albert. If he's got a fault, it is that he tends to be too rigid. Take, for example . . .'

I heard my own voice slur to a halt. In the act of turning my head to monitor progress on the beef sandwiches, I had obtained a brief view down the length of the room via a mirror above the bar. On the further shores of a sea of milling figures, one head in particular had stood out for that moment. It wore a circular yellow woollen hat. When I twisted on the stool to look direct the throng had rearranged itself to obscure my sightline. I craned my neck, seeking a fresh angle.

Spalding's voice said, 'Seen someone you know?'

With an effort I returned to him. 'Nobody of importance.'

'She might quarrel with that assessment,' he said archly.

'Hang on a minute.' I got to my feet. 'I'll just fetch my sandwiches.'

Returning to the other end of the counter, I stood with my back to it, staring between heads. Presently I started working my way around the perimeter of the room, having to weave among tables, step over legs. I caught one glimpse of Spalding: he had buttonholed someone else and was emphasizing a point with finger-stabs. Arriving at the far end of the room, I found myself in the thick of a large group who were arguing about interest rates. It took me a while to extricate myself. When I emerged, the placidity of a remote corner was there to welcome me. Of padded jacket or woollen hat there was no trace.

Then I spotted him again. He was standing by the counter, not far from the point I had just left. A pint tankard rested against his left palm, but he wasn't drinking. He was looking down the room, not at me — not at anyone specifically — with a detached unblinking gaze reminiscent of a hotel commissionaire trying to avoid being asked the way to somewhere.

The part I could see of him reminded me of a bust of Beethoven. Brute power showed in the features. He was tall, strongly built, altogether formidable. The Muldoon patrons flanking him looked puny by contrast. Given the incentive he could, I felt, have flicked the lot of them aside with one hand, clearing a path straight towards me . . .

Depositing my glass on the shelf of a nearby radiator, I headed for the exit.

Back on the street, I stepped out briskly. The office was only a few blocks away. Passing a news kiosk, I noticed a change of headline on a display of one of the evening papers: the second edition was on sale. After a hesitant look behind, I stopped and asked for a copy of each. I had to wait while the gnome of a newsvendor, his arthritic fingers semi-encased in fleece-lined plastic, fumbled out change for a pound note. As he chanted it into my hand, I glanced back again. A few hats were in sight, but nothing of the tea-cosy species. I relaxed slightly.

'There y'are, guv. They've killed 'im orff, I see.'

'What?'

The newsvendor completed his insertion of my pound note into the lining of his cap, which lay top down on his stand. 'Bishop's Lad. Going too hard, they say. Fair old excuse if you ask me. He weren't up to the weight, that's the truth of it.'

'Right,' I said knowingly. I cared nothing about racing, and knew less. Moving away a few yards, I carried out a quick scan of both front and back pages. The bulk of the news was identical to that carried in the first editions, with craftily amended headings. The main fresh item concerned an enquiry into the route of a planned motorway. The Stop Press contained nothing of interest.

From outside the office entrance I glanced back once more along the street. There was no sign of blue or yellow.

Amanda was finishing a call. Waiting until the phone went down, I said, 'No luck yet?'

'No luck, period.' She leaned back, stretching herself and yawning. 'Stuffy in here,' she complained. 'I've rung them all, Mr Cassell, but nobody's seen him. You were quick.'

'I wasn't hungry. Nowhere else we can try?'

She pondered. 'What's the name of that club he belongs to? He might have gone there for lunch.'

'The Repton? He went off the place. But it's worth a bash. After that, Amanda, you might put a call through to his sister in Reigate. It's just feasible he had some kind of an SOS from her and went scooting off down there. I'll let you have the number.'

Leaving her dialling, I shut myself into the main office and moved cautiously towards the window. Before I got there, I could see that he was back. Same position, same attitude; the steady gaze that was not a scrutiny. For a while I watched him, no longer bothering to conceal myself. He gave no indication that I was visible to him. His posture betrayed nothing. He might have been a stone appendage of the building.

Amanda came in. 'They hardly seemed to have heard of him at the club. They did page him, but no joy. His sister's out, but according to some guy who said he was from the Gas Board she's only gone shopping and he's expecting her back any time. He certainly didn't know of any emergency—apart from a new pump needed on the boiler. Shall I try again later?'

I huffed out some breath. 'You might as well. Though I think we're wasting our time.'

'Where do you think he's gone?' she asked curiously.

'If I knew that, I wouldn't be asking you to phone around.'

'I just wondered if you'd any ideas,' she said meekly.

'Sorry, Amanda. No, I haven't. I'm a bit worried.'

'But he's gone off before, hasn't he, without leaving an itinerary?'

'We've known he was off on his rounds,' I pointed out. 'Whereas this morning, he was simply intending to fetch his car and come back here. An hour, at the most. He's been gone four.'

A thought seemed to hit her. 'Shouldn't we—?'

'I already have,' I said hurriedly. 'They shoved me around a bit between departments, so I gave up. But in any case, even if they could tell us the car's been collected, where does that get us? They wouldn't have a clue where he went afterwards, any more than we do.'

'But if there's been an accident . . .'

'In that event, the obvious person to contact is his wife. She'd have been notified. I might call her again in a little while.'

Amanda wandered past me towards the window. 'It's so unlike Mr Hall,' she observed, peering out, 'to leave us guessing like this. I do hope nothing's happened. I thought he'd been looking rather uptight lately. Tense. Did you get that impression?'

'He's not exactly the relaxed type.'

'No, but just in the last week or two . . . There are some weird characters around, aren't there?'

'I'm sorry?'

'There's some yobbo taken root in the entrance to Copperton's over the road. I noticed him once or twice before lunch. And he's still there, would you believe?'

I said off-handedly, 'Killing time, no doubt, till he can pick up his next social security handout.'

'Funny place to wait.'

'One's as good as another. You were saying, you thought Mr Hall had been looking . . . strung up?'

With a final glance through the window she returned to where I was standing and lowered her voice. 'I didn't like to mention it to anyone, but I definitely had the idea his mind wasn't on his work. He seemed jumpy and he wasn't concentrating. While he was dictating, he kept on sort of drifting away, losing the thread. Know what I mean?'

'Yes. I think I do.' I was also aware, acutely, of something else: the unwontedly close proximity of Amanda and the size of her eyes, which were fixed upon mine with a naive conjecture that I found disturbing. If Albert had been apt to lose the thread, I reflected, the cause might not be hard to determine. When she tried—or perhaps, more accurately, when she didn't try—Amanda was capable of radiating her share of feminine appeal: could its cumulative effect have thrown my partner off balance? Knowing his susceptibilities, I was not prepared to write off the hypothesis. In my own case, abundantly provided for as I was in the sphere of female consolation, the allure of our shared secretary was something I had never found it hard to resist. Now, abruptly, I was seeing her in a fresh light. Poor old Albert. Was it conceivable . . . ?

Moving clear, I said crisply, 'Give me an outside line, Amanda, will you?'

She left the door ajar. I nudged it shut before returning to my desk, lifting the receiver and dialling. A good part of my working life was spent in the performance of these simple actions. Until today, I had never paused to ask myself how business would be conducted without the magic speaking device that everyone took for granted. An inestimable service Edison had provided. People said it was television that revolutionized the world: my personal view was that the telephone had done the job already, years ahead. And here we all were, throwing our voices at each other across fathomless gulfs, annoyed when a wrong connection delayed us for thirty seconds. The subject was worthy of a thesis. I wondered why I was giving thought to it.

'Mel? Steve, yet again. Still no sign of Albo?'

'He hasn't floated past the window on his umbrella, if that's what you mean. You seem to be getting frightfully het up about him. He's vanished before.'

'Not like this. We've always had a rough idea what he was planning to do.'

'You think he might have made off with the profits?'

'The point is,' I said, ignoring her remark, 'he had a rather broken night, as I mentioned. He may not have been too co-ordinated when he picked up his car.'

'Have you rung the police?'

'I thought I'd check with you again first. If anything had happened they'd have been in touch with you, wouldn't they?'

'Presumably.' She sounded bored. 'In technical terms, I suppose I'm the person to acquaint with any disaster. Well, I've been here most of the day and I've heard from no one—except you. Oh, there was a call about twelve, twelve-fifteen . . . soon after you called last time. But when I answered there was dead silence, so I hung up. That wasn't you?'

'No. Outside call?'

'From a call box? I've no way of knowing.'

'If it had been, you'd have heard pips.'

'Mm.' After a short pause she spoke again, more sharply. 'You really are making a big deal of this. You know damn well we hardly see each other, Albo and I. When he *is* here, he does have the decency to keep out of my way. Why would I suddenly be familiar with his movements? Far as I'm concerned, he just gets on with it. I thought that was the way you operated, the two of you.'

'Up to a point.' I hesitated. 'Circumstances this time are a little different, that's all. Maybe I'm getting worked up for no reason.'

'I should call the police.'

'You will get in touch if he shows up?'

'I'll be in touch.' Her phone went down.

Remaining in the chair, I kept one hand on the receiver rest while continuing to hold the receiver with the other and frowning at the window. From this position I couldn't see to street level. All I could make out were streaks on the panes, indicating the onset of rain. I prayed for a squall of some ferocity. Thigh-length jackets and woollen hats were poor protection against torrents. Lifting my right hand, I regained the dialling tone. Amanda, smart girl, had left the line open. The dial whirred under my finger.

'Police? I wonder if you can help me. I want to make an enquiry . . .'

'What's it in connection with, sir?'

'It's a sort of a missing person matter.'

'Putting you through.'

The rain streaks were starting to blanket the window. They were being blown against the glass in salvoes. The sky had darkened.

A new voice asked if it could help me.

'I'm not sure. I want to make a fairly tentative enquiry about someone who . . . hasn't turned up for an appointment. I don't want to waste your time, but—'

'Name of the person, sir?'

'Actually, I just wanted your advice as to whether you think I'm panicking too soon. It's only a matter of a few hours, you see. Seems premature to report him missing. But if he'd been involved in an accident or something, do you think I'd have heard by now?'

'That all depends. How overdue is he?'

'Something over four hours.'

'How far did he have to travel? Are you in London?'

'Yes. He was only coming a few miles.'

'Are you related, sir?'

'No. Just business associates.'

'Does he have any family? Have you contacted anyone?'

'I've phoned around, but no one seems to have seen

him. Assuming an accident—'

'If the gentleman's been hurt, sir, and taken to hospital, one of the police officers dealing with the incident would have seen to it that next of kin were notified. Assuming he could be identified. You wouldn't care to give me his name?'

'I'd prefer not, at the moment. I might cause needless alarm. You do understand?'

'I wouldn't worry unduly,' said the voice with a comfortable impassivity. 'If it were an accident, I think word would have trickled through to you by now. More likely something unexpected came up and he's not been able to get to a telephone.'

'I'm sure you're right.'

'Call us back if you think we can help further.'

'Thank you, I will.'

Rain lashed the panes. Cradling the phone, I switched on the desk lamp, spotlighting the abandoned mail lying in heaps. Chin in hand, I stared past it at the dense gloom outside. By now, I thought, the gutters would be running.

Presently I rose and walked to the window.

Vision was obscured, but I could see that lights had come on inside the Copperton building opposite. The main street entrance, too, was brightly lit, casting its radiance on the rain-cleared pavement. At the top of the steps, something circular and yellow stood out in the refulgence. It was close to the left-hand wall, sheltered from wind and moisture. I gave it one hard look and turned away.

Amanda was typing. She completed a sentence before looking up with the large eyes. 'What a storm! Shall I get through to Reigate now, Mr Cassell?'

'I've spoken to the police,' I told her. 'They seem to think there'll be a perfectly simple explanation—which is obviously the case. The fact remains . . . Yes, you may as well try his sister again. Any chance of some tea?'

'I'll make it as soon as I've rung.'

I hung around while she made the call. When she said, 'Oh, Mrs Peterson, it's Amanda Barnes, your brother's secretary . . .' I saw Clare vividly at the telephone stand, clear-eyed, permed and groomed, encircled by children and pets, competently in command of events, untroubled by the recollection that in addition to a secretary her brother had a partner. Amanda said, 'Yes, I'm fine. Family all keeping well? That's good. I'm only ringing to ask whether you've seen your brother today, at all? No, we're just trying to trace him. He went off without leaving a message, which is unusual. Please, if you would. We'd be so grateful. Pretty busy, thanks. All right, then. 'Bye.' She disconnected. 'He hasn't been there, either.'

'I never imagined he had.'

I found myself pacing the room in circles, like an expectant father; all that was lacking was a trail of cigarette butts. At times like this, I vaguely regretted not being a smoker. Although I kept a stock of filter-tips at home, they were not for myself.

On the other hand, a time like this had never previously cropped up. Not precisely like this. It ran beyond the compass of my experience: I was having to improvise. A call from an irate lawyer on behalf of an aggrieved client—that I could have dealt with. This was tantamount to punching at mist.

I became aware of Amanda's half-frowning inspection. Meeting my eye, she gave a quick smile. 'Shall I get the tea now?'

I nodded. 'Make enough for three. He might show up any minute.'

CHAPTER 6

Driving home, I caught myself keeping an almost non-stop check on the rear-view mirror.

Traffic was well up to peak-hour capacity, but this hardly accounted for an obsessive preoccupation with what was happening to my rear. I forced myself to look ahead, to behave like a home-bound commuter with a few office worries still fermenting in his brain. Within a few moments the pretence sputtered and died. I was back to the flickering-gaze syndrome, the restless observation that spelt uncertainty. Curiosity. That was the better word. It avoided overstating the case.

Passing the Law Courts, I was overtaken by a cab that had been dogging me for a mile or more. Another took its place. It pursued me up Ludgate Hill, tailed me towards the Barbican, finally shook itself off like a dead leaf at an intersection and dropped back out of sight as I came within range of the ramp to my garage. On impulse I drove past, circled the block, approached the ramp a second time.

When I reached the concrete basement I was unaccompanied. The barrier lifted itself lazily, like the exploring neck of a giraffe, as I fed it my plastic card. Driving into my bay, I got out and double-checked the security of every door of the car before making for the lift.

There was nothing wayward about most of this. I did it every working evening—except the double approach. This was new, and something I couldn't explain, even to myself. Thinking it over as I soared, I concluded I must have been travelling too fast the first time to make a comfortable sweep on to the ramp. That was it. In any case, it wasn't important. The only reason I was thinking about it at all was that, to the average balanced realist, explicability is nice to have: not a matter of life or death, just an amenity.

Stepping clear of the lift, I remembered there was one place I had failed to check during the day.

I almost ran the rest of the way to my apartment door. Now that the notion had struck me, I was convinced it must be right. Some time in the forgotten past—or possibly last night—Albert must have acquired a key to my residence and now, for reasons of his own, he was making use of it. Why should he seek the refuge of my rooms? Because he was scared: that was why. Petrified of being picked up.

The TV would be on, that was for sure. Radio, too. Albert wouldn't be missing a newscast if he could help it. But unless there had been some development since the final editions of the evening papers, he couldn't have learned much.

Silence greeted me as I unlatched the door.

So complete had been my certainty that, for a moment, I stood in a state of disbelief at the entrance to the living-room, adjusting to the inescapable fact that my partner was not among its contents. An inspection of the other rooms yielded the same finding. The bed on which Albert had slept the night before was still a little crumpled: that and a misplaced cushion on one of the living-room chairs were the sole indications that he had ever been around. Depositing my briefcase, I stood meditating.

Presently I switched on the TV. A tribe of naked Africans were chanting at a coal-black figure dressed in a pinstripe suit as he waved to them from the fuselage door of a DC10. 'Self-determination,' the voice-over was intoning, 'is the dream of Mr Mugomo's people: his mission now . . .' Keeping an eye on the screen, I removed my outer coat and flung it over a chair-back before reducing the sound a little and walking over to where the radio stood at one end of the dresser. I was reaching for the on-button when the telephone rang.

Hurrying across the room, I snatched up the receiver. 'Yes, who is it?'

'I'm speaking on behalf of Mr Hall.'

I let a second or two elapse. 'Did you call me before?'

'If you remember, I did mention you'd be hearing from me again. Have you anything to tell me?'

'Look, I don't mean to be rude, but if you expect any help from me you'll have to explain yourself a little. Without knowing your name, your relationship to—'

'It's not that I *expect* help, Mr Cassell. I was hoping you might have decided at least not to be obstructive. Finchley isn't far, remember. Less than half an hour by car . . . wouldn't you say?'

'What the hell are you on about?'

'Accidents can't be avoided, but there are certain events . . . We don't want to harp on them, do we?'

'I don't want to harp on anything. Since you refuse to announce yourself or talk sense, we've nothing to discuss. How did you—'

'Later, perhaps. I'll call back.'

'Wait a bit.' The ballpen I was toying with broke in my fingers. Stupidly I watched the two pieces hit the carpet, the ink stain soak into my index finger. 'I can't guess what you're up to. But I'm not having you repeat this performance whenever you feel inclined. We'll thrash it out now, do you hear? If you've information concerning my partner—'

'No no, you misunderstand. It's information from you I want.'

'*What* information, for Christ's sake?'

'Speak to you again, Mr Cassell. 'Bye for now.'

The line clicked.

Kneeling, I retrieved the halves of ballpen, placed them alongside the phone directories. While I was searching the carpet pile for stray particles I realized that the receiver had remained in my hand. Mechanically I steered it back on to its rest. I stood up, dusting my hands, and gazed at the TV screen. It was now showing a London street, identifiable as such by the red double-decker bus vanishing around a curve. At centre of the picture, a pair of police officers stood beside a patrol car. One of them seemed to be using his personal radio. I turned up the sound.

'... keeping a low profile,' the newscaster was saying, 'in what amounts to a test of mutual tolerance between, on the one hand, a law enforcement squad with hazily defined terms of reference and, on the other, a work force who have come to regard industrial action as a sacred ...'

Subsiding into the sprung well of a chair, I let the phrases wash over me like the bars of a familiar piece of middlebrow music, while my brain revolved, active, ineffectual, taking me nowhere.

When I next took note of the screen, a girl with wind-blown hair was recounting, from the battlements, the history of a Kent castle threatened by a road scheme. In a vague way, she reminded me of someone. Her place was taken by a male spokesman for the local authority and I rose, again subdued the sound while retaining the picture, returned to the telephone and made a call.

Feeling better when I hung up, I poured myself a brandy, drank it, measured another. The effect of the twin dose was to remind me that I had barely eaten since breakfast. Apart from a biscuit with my afternoon tea, food had seemed more irrelevant than usual to the proceedings at the office, such as they were. Appetite still eluded me. At the same time, I suspected that starvation was not helping my efficiency. Inside a kitchen cupboard I found a hunk of madeira cake from which I sliced half an inch. Taking it back to the living-room on a saucer, I opened my briefcase and extracted the final editions I had bought on the way home. With half an eye to the screen I papered the coffee table, bit off a zestless mouthful of cake and began turning the pages.

The door buzzer bleated.

Surprised, I glanced at my watch. Swallowing the mouthful, I strode out to the lobby. As I opened the door I said, 'You didn't waste any—'

'Mr Cassell?'

I gave the blue padded jacket a long, silent survey. The yellow woollen hat was balled into one of the hip pockets; an edge protruded. At close quarters he was larger than ever. He belonged to a rugby pack. I held the door where it had come to rest.

'I'm sorry . . . I was expecting someone else. Something I can do for you?'

'We can talk about it better inside.' He spoke with a soft courtesy that made nonsense of his physical demeanour.

'It's just as easy to talk here. What do you want?'

'I'd like,' he said, 'to know the way to Finchley.'

After a space I stepped back, taking the door with me. 'Come on in.'

Establishing himself in an easy upright posture at the centre of the living-room, he took in the surroundings with the practised air of an estate agent. He had a snub nose and an upturned chin, which between them gave a squashed look to his face. With an assumption of idle curiosity I leaned against the dresser.

'What's this all about?'

His head rotated back to me. There was a squinting appearance to his eyes, as though too many months and years of sustained observation had resulted in retinal damage. After a brief look, his glance slid away from me again. The Stubbs picture in the alcove seemed to have captured his attention.

I said, 'You've been tailing me, haven't you?'

He replied mildly, 'I was hoping you might be able to show me the way to Finchley.'

'What's all this claptrap about Finchley?'

'You tell me.' He spoke with an air of agreeably vehement candour.

'Who the devil are you? I want to know your name and I want to know why you're here.'

'I'm a thug,' he said cheerily. 'I've come to mug you and lift a few oddments.'

'You could be, at that.'

'Why let me in, then?'

I regarded him silently. He was still appraising the Stubbs; advancing a pace or two, peering, stepping back for a fresh look.

'I've had a couple of peculiar phone calls today,' I said. 'Not you, by any chance?'

He blinked. 'Did it sound like me?'

'It sounded like a woman.'

'Do I sound like a woman?'

'You could be a master of vocal disguise.'

He smiled, appreciating the phrase. 'Yes, I might, mightn't I? There's no telling.'

'There certainly isn't. No one seems inclined to tell me anything that makes a morsel of sense. I think I must ask you to leave.'

'Are you asking me?'

'If you like.'

'It's not what I like, Mr Cassell. Very largely I'm in your hands. If you want me to go, I'll go.'

'I do want you to.'

'Okay.' He started for the door.

'But not,' I added, arresting him halfway, 'before you've explained yourself a bit. I think I've a right to know what you're up to. You seem to be acquainted with me, but I'm damned if I can say the same about you.'

'I thought you said you'd seen me before.'

'You know bloody well what I mean.'

He studied me broodingly. 'I can see I'm starting to get on your nerves. Know what I'd do, in your position?'

'Do enlighten me.'

'I'd chuck me out. Or else I'd call the cops, get them to do it for me.'

'Don't tempt me.'

A frown crushed his features still more comprehensively. 'Not sure I understand you, Mr Cassell. You don't seem to react in the way I'd expect.'

'How do you mean?'

'I'm not trying to tempt you to do anything. I'm offering rational advice which you're quite at liberty to act on. I mean, I can see your point. I am intruding. I am being cagey. You do have the right to see me off the premises. What's stopping you?'

I changed position against the dresser, hooking one leg carelessly about the other.

'Call it vulgar inquisitiveness. I'm intrigued to know what it is about me that's held you spellbound all day. Nothing odd about that reaction, I'd have thought.'

He gave the matter some consideration. His gaze wandered towards the coffee table. He nodded at it. 'Keen reader of the evening Press, I see.'

'I try to keep up with the news.'

'Should think you manage all right. You've left the TV on, did you know?'

'Yes. I was interrupted.'

His eyes skidded on to the dresser behind me. 'Transistor, too. You do keep yourself informed. Much of interest occurred recently?'

Detaching myself from the dresser, I turned the TV off. 'Why don't you take a seat?' I enquired. 'If we're going to fence, we may as well do it in comfort. Care for a drink?'

Installing himself with deliberation in a mahogany-armed chair that growled under his weight, he shook his head. 'Not for me. But don't let me stop you. Oh, you're provided for, I see. Feel in need of a bracer, I dare say.'

'Why do you say that?'

'After a hectic day,' he explained, 'at the office.'

'It has been a little fraught.'

'Go on?'

'No—*you* go on. I'm still waiting for an explanation.'

'What of? My interest in you?'

'What else?'

'I thought possibly you might have been wondering about your partner.'

Keeping the brandy glass steady, I examined it closely. 'Wondering about him?'

'Yes. Speculating.'

'Why should I want to do that?'

He said nothing. Since seating himself, he had seemed preoccupied with the stowage of limbs in a confined space; now, for the first time, his eyes became fixed upon me in a level inspection that was neither malignant nor benign. It was the gaze of a security officer watching a monitor screen in a department store.

'What do you know about my partner, anyhow? Are you a friend of his?'

'Friends.' He weighed the word. 'There aren't too many people,' he said eventually, 'I could honestly describe as that.'

I put the glass down. 'Look, Mr Whoever-you-are. I think it's time we came off the ice. I'm going to assume you know what's happened: that my partner's gone missing and I'm worried about him. Now then. Is there some information you can give me?'

'You've reported him missing? To the police?'

'No, I haven't.'

'Why not?'

'It seemed premature.'

'But you say you're worried about him.'

'That's not the same as . . . It's not strictly up to me. He's got a wife. She'll no doubt report it if necessary.'

'When will it become necessary?'

'That remains to be seen.'

His gaze drifted to the ceiling. 'I'd have thought,' he said abstractedly, 'you'd at least have *mentioned* it to the police by now.'

After an interval I said, 'Right. Cards face up on the table. Are you the spokesman for a bunch of kidnappers?'

He continued to study the plasterwork.

'If it's money you want,' I said, keeping my temper in check, 'why can't you just come out with it, instead of playing this cat-and-mouse game? Do you find it amusing?'

'Speaking of money,' he said, blinking at me, 'you don't do so badly, Mr Cassell, you and your partner. Am I right? Prosperous business you've worked up there. Healthy profits.'

'We're nothing like as loaded as you might—'

'Oh, I understand. Easy to grab the wrong impression. Big difference between pre-tax and after-tax . . . one appreciates that.'

'All companies are on the same treadmill.'

He nodded slowly. 'That's true, I guess, to some extent.'

I glanced at him sharply. 'What are you getting at?'

'Some firms are better placed than others, aren't they? For mitigating the burden?' He spread a hand self-deprecatingly. 'Not that I'm up in these matters.'

I sat back. 'Nevertheless, you seem to be implying something.'

'I'm just a mouthpiece. You mustn't take too much notice of what I say.'

'You wouldn't by any chance be an inspector from the Inland Revenue?'

'Assuming I was,' he said delicately, 'would you be bothered?'

'Let's say I'd find it tiresome. One never exactly welcomes the attentions of such visitors.'

'But would they *agitate* you?'

'Without knowing more about you, I don't think I feel disposed to answer any more of your impudent questions. We've got off the subject of Mr Hall. That's the one that concerns me.'

'Of course. And you never answered my original impudent question.'

'Which one's that?'

'The best way to get to Finchley.'

'I don't know how to answer it.'

'It's a straightforward query. What's the problem?'

'I can't make out if you're trying to tell me something.'

He shrugged. 'It's funny. You don't seem to respond to an ordinary enquiry in the way that anyone else would. In fact, I can't see much point in protracting this discussion. Sorry to have troubled you, Mr Cassell. I'll be on my way.'

'Wait!' He hovered in a semi-upright position. 'You can't leave,' I said urgently, 'just like that. There are too many loose ends. I don't know where I stand. You've got my partner—is this what you're saying? You want money for him? I have to know.'

He finalized his knee-straightening programme. 'Why?'

'Why? For God's sake. What do you take me for?'

'A reasonable sort of guy. I approach most people on that assumption,' he informed me, extracting his woolly hat and jamming it carefully over his wiry black hair so that it sat on his ears. 'I take common sense and co-operation very largely for granted, and I'm bound to say I'm not often disappointed. Quite rarely. Says something, doesn't it, for human nature? It's very heartening.'

'Co-operation? Is that what you're demanding of me?'

He paused on his way to the door. 'I wouldn't like to

think I was making *demands* on anyone.' He sounded reproachful. 'Not my style at all.'

'So what is your style? Tell me. Let me know what I have to do.'

From the doorway, he looked back. 'I should do whatever you think best, Mr Cassell. That's my advice.'

CHAPTER 7

I made another phone call.

This time there was no reply. I hung on until the ringing tone lost its voice, then furiously slammed down the receiver and went to the window. By now it was dark outside, but the street below was brilliantly lit, and manifestly unpopulated. Scanning it as thoroughly as I could, I concluded that if Padded Jacket had resumed a waiting stance he was being untypically coy about it. There seemed no reason for a sudden switch of policy on his part. Up to now, concealment had plainly been the last consideration in his mind.

On the other hand, there might be an exceedingly good reason.

I was party to nothing. Whatever was going on, nobody was continually panting up to me with explanations. I was having to grope. Reason, just now, scarcely figured on the scene.

Abandoning the window, I got back into my shoes and put on my coat.

Before leaving the apartment, I dialled again and waited. No answer.

The car's engine, still slightly warm, fired instantly, uproarious in the ferro-concrete cavern of the garage. I drove out cautiously, taking the ramp to street level in bottom gear.

At the entrance to the roadway I braked, peering both ways. The glare from the colonnaded lamps showed me a harsh landscape of asphalt and paving and little else, apart from Doug's news-stand, shuttered for the night, a homely wart on the Barbican's haughty flesh. In the wake of the business rush, the street looked like an East Coast beach on an ebbing tide. Accelerating hard, I took off to my right.

For the first mile I drove like a lunatic, disregarding speed limits, throwing the car Keystone Cops-style around corners, until I felt reasonably certain that nothing was on my tail or that, if it had been, I had shaken it off. After that I cruised more soberly. The legacy of the day's downpour was beginning to dry out, but wet patches remained and the general effect was more than ever of a deserted coastline. The City at night: a pleasant haven of inactivity, I had always thought. Other descriptions occurred to me now.

Reviewing the encounter with Padded Jacket, I felt dimly convinced there was more I could have said. Why hadn't I asserted myself? I should have insisted on knowing his name. Kept him there until he stopped talking in riddles. Demanded to know what had become of Albert. Required a price.

What had stopped me?

It was like looking back on a verbal insult. Anyone can think of half a dozen crushing retorts . . . too late. The trick is to have one handy at the time, primed for projection. In my case, nothing had been ready. I was caught off-guard, as I had been all day.

Albert's flat was on the first floor of a mansion block on the Chelsea Embankment. It owed nothing to Newstyle Properties. He and Melanie had chosen it before their marriage, and my only involvement had been to advance him a fair slice of the purchase capital at a derisory interest rate: he had since repaid me prematurely, in full. Albert loathed debt.

Driving beside the river towards the block, I wondered what he now thought of his investment. It was occupied by a wife who had lost whatever interest she had ever had in him, and if they split up she would get half, at least. During the week, when he made some use of the place as a dormitory, they barely met. At weekends he had got into the habit of visiting Clare at Reigate, where there was an openended welcome for him. Or so he had given me to understand.

Stronger than the renewed gust of sympathy for Albert that rocked me was the combination of apprehension and perplexity arising out of the events of the past twenty-four hours. What kind of mess had my partner landed himself in? I had to know.

Standing some way back from the river behind lawns and shrubs and flowering cherry trees which as yet boasted neither blossom nor foliage, the apartment block was reached by a tarmac drive leading straight to the main entrance. Albert's flat overlooked it. As I drove up, I could see at a glance that there was no light behind any of the windows. Applying the handbrake, I climbed out and hurried through the jabbing claws of the breeze into the relative serenity of the building, ignoring the lift and taking the single flight of carpeted stairs to the first floor.

My pressure on the bell-push inspired a dual-tone 'Gong-gong' from inside the apartment; and nothing else. I waited; tried again. No result.

Walking across to the single door on the opposite side of the landing, I rang there.

A voice said in my ear, 'Who is it?'

'A friend of Mr and Mrs Hall,' I told the entryphone. 'Name of Cassell.'

'The Halls live opposite. Number Five.'

'Yes, I'm aware of that. I've rung and there's no answer. You don't happen to know where they might be?'

'I've no idea.' The voice was discernibly female, and ready to break contact.

'Is there anybody else living here that I might ask?'

Pause. 'I really couldn't say. I doubt if anyone would be familiar with their hour-to-hour movements. Were they expecting you?'

'It's looking less and less like it,' I said. 'Thank you for your help.'

The entryphone made no further comment. Walking back downstairs I stood just inside the entrance, surveying the semi-darkness outside. Nobody came or went. There was no sign of a porter. From the river a few lights were faintly visible beyond the more immediate activity on the Embankment. I pushed my way out through the revolving doors and re-entered the car.

The fascia clock indicated nearly seven thirty. Swinging the car round, I rejoined the motorized stampede in an easterly direction for a short distance before bearing left towards Victoria.

Rain attacked again, battering the windscreen in a fury. The wipers at top speed could barely cope with it. Fumbling with the ventilation controls, I inadvertently flicked on the radio, in time to catch the tag end of a news bulletin: '. . . charge of investigations, Chief Superintendent Edgar White, said that house-to-house enquiries were being pursued in the district and that a number of other possible leads were being followed up. The man they were looking for, he added, was undoubtedly dangerous, and he warned against attempts by members of the public to detain him. That's it for now, back to the music. Among our galaxy of hit singles from the Seventies—'

Savagely I switched to another station, and another. No rival bulletins were being broadcast except on a French waveband, at such a pace that I could only guess wildly at the content: it seemed to have something to do with events of a diplomatic nature in Paris. When I had exhausted the wavelengths I returned to the original programme, endured a succession of tribal numbers while blazing a route through the West End theatre traffic. By the time I achieved the more placid latitudes of St John's Wood and Swiss Cottage I had listened to enough punk rock to explode the eardrums of a deaf Sealyham, but I had heard no further newscast.

My attention began to desert the radio in favour of my surroundings. I was approaching the district where I had picked up Albert the previous night. It was still relatively unfamiliar to me and I had to concentrate. Luckily the rain had slackened. The odd flurry swooped, but mostly it was being dissipated by the wind. I could see my way without difficulty. The call box was closer to the junction than I remembered, but it served to orientate me, and having taken stock for a few moments I puttered on slowly, swung left and then right, continued along the course we had taken on foot.

It was simpler than I had feared. Having retained in my memory most of the features we had passed, I had only to navigate from one to the next, until an illuminated shop-window seized my eye. J. Barnsley, Newsagent and Confectioner. I was practically there.

The car went smoothly into the final corner.

I drove to the far end of the street with my head motionless, only my eyes swivelling as I passed the converted cottage. There was little to be seen. Just the blank frontage: no trace of light. On either side, similar properties, with here and there a glow behind curtains. There were no spaces between the vehicles parked at the kerbside. And not a pedestrian in sight. By eight o'clock of a wet evening the bolts in this street, as in most others, were shot for the night.

Turning at the end, a cul-de-sac, I cruised back, and

passed closer to the cottage. No hint of activity came from it; nothing to indicate that the place had drawn any more attention than it had the previous night when Albert and I had made our confused exits, jamming the street door behind us. It looked, in all conscience, like a hundred other residences within a radius of half a mile.

Turning left into the main road, I allowed the car to roll in neutral down the gradient, passed by other traffic, until it chuntered to a halt almost outside J. Barnsley, Newsagent and Confectioner, which was closed for the night. The pavement at this point performed a wriggle, providing the semblance of a lay-by for wheelborne customers—strictly an illegal facility, to judge from the yellow band markings, but one that had all the appearance of semi-official sanction. Nudging the car into the bulge, I parked it there.

Having secured the doors, I walked back uphill to the junction.

There, for several minutes, I wavered. Then I started walking again, chiefly because I felt conspicuous in a pool of artificial light at the corner, and once I was on my way along the street itself there was no turning back. I had to reach that front door.

It sat stolidly in its frame, lumpish, opaque, its glazed strip revealing nothing. Standing before it, I felt like a postman who had lost his mail sack. From somewhere, I was convinced, I was being watched. Assessed. Not a good feeling. My upper arms tingled, anticipating sudden seizure from behind. I felt horribly prominent, there on the narrow footway, gazing at a door. I could turn and retreat, or . . .

Extending a hand, I gave the woodwork a push.

It shuddered at the base, but the top corner remained stuck. With my palm I administered a smart tap. The door bounced clear.

Nothing I had ever attempted came within hailing distance of a comparison with the action of stepping across that doorstep into the gloom beyond. Once through, I found myself incapable of further movement. My brain shut down.

The drift of the door past my left shoulder got me mobile again. It missed me narrowly before reconnecting with a low thud that echoed around the walls. After that, I could hear my own breathing but I could see nothing, and for the second time my muscles froze. Providentially, a motor-cycle roared past outside, the mental electro-therapy of the outburst impelling me once more into motion, taking me through the inner door which, as before, yielded to my advance. As before, the room lay in darkness until I found the switch.

The mental image I had carried for a day proved accurate. To my right was the kitchen door, half open as we had left it. A corner of the living-room's central rug had been kicked back: I remembered doing that as Albert bundled me out of the place in hysterics. This apart, there was no sign of disturbance.

Hovering by the kitchen doorway, I tried to think clinically.

If nothing had yet been discovered, Albert for the moment remained in the clear. This, in turn, meant that I had no immediate worries on that score. All I needed to do was trace the whereabouts of Albert.

And find out where Padded Jacket fitted in. To say nothing of the phone calls.

In the entire room, the only things that moved were the hands of the electric clock. Their latest jerk had taken them on to eight twenty-three.

Time was passing. With a sudden kick I sent the kitchen door back to its limit, stepped past it and switched on the overhead light.

The sink was empty. I had time to notice this before the figure on the floor captured my attention. It lay in a huddled position beneath a worktop, face down; but there was no need to turn it over, even if I had felt inclined. All too clearly, the red-stained body was that of Albert.

CHAPTER 8

'Your name, sir?'
'Cassell. Stephen Cassell.'
'And you wish to report an accident?'
'I think so.'
'Beg pardon, sir?'
'I mean it could be something . . . rather more serious. A killing.'
'Where are you speaking from?'
'A telephone kiosk. It's at . . .' Hesitantly in the half-light, I read out the name of the road. 'Quite near where I've just come from.'
'And where's that, Mr Cassell?'
I gave him the address. 'Shall I get back there now?'
'If you don't mind. Someone will be with you very shortly. By yourself, sir?'
'Yes.'
'Have you alerted anyone else? Neighbours?'
'Not yet.'
'Then please don't. Do nothing until the police arrive. Don't touch anything.'
'I wasn't going to. Shall I wait outside the house?'
'If you can, without attracting attention. One thing, Mr Cassell. You're certain the person concerned is dead?'
'Absolutely.'
'All right. Get back to the house and wait there.'
I left the call box and set off back. In my search for a telephone I had come farther than I had realized: the

return trip was a good half-mile, largely uphill and against the wind. I felt at the end of my endurance. On the way down, I had been in a spinning world of my own; returning, with the news of Albert's demise offloaded to a neutral voice, in the knowledge that official wheels were starting to turn, I experienced an overwhelming reaction. The route seemed endless. Rain was still flecking the air. Finchley, I resolved, could manage without me in future. When this was over, it would take something like an oil strike to entice me within its boundaries again.

Thoughts about Albert kept pumping through my brain.

Without a doubt, the poor bastard had belonged to the category of the accident-prone. His personality had seemed to lure disaster. And now it looked as if even his death was going to be thoroughly inexplicable. The police were going to have problems with this one.

When I arrived back at the cottage they were already there. Two of them. In the absence of kerb space, their car had been left at the centre of the road: its lights had been switched off, and the roof-mounted blue lamp lay dormant. Evidently they had no wish to arouse the neighbourhood. As I came along, one of them was cautiously trying the street door, which I had taken care to drag shut behind me. Catching their attention, I managed a weary trot for the last few yards.

'I'm Stephen Cassell.' Conforming to their low-key approach, I kept my voice down. 'I've just reported the incident. The door opens if you lean on it. The catch doesn't fasten.'

'I see,' the leading one said noncommittally. The door swung inwards to a biff from his forearm. 'Perhaps you'd like to wait here, Mr Cassell, with my colleague, Police Constable Ward. I'll just take a look. Where exactly . . . ?'

I described the location of the kitchen. 'It's my partner, Mr Hall. I found him there when I arrived.'

He stepped into the hallway and after a moment found the light switch. The door shut itself behind him. Constable Ward, tall and incredibly young, stood regarding it with manifest disquiet before turning to me.

'Messy?' he asked on a note of uneasiness.

'A little, I'm afraid. There was blood on the back of his head, and on his shoulders. And some spots over the floor.'

He swallowed. 'My stomach's not all that strong. You didn't try to move him?'

'I just shook him gently by the shoulder. He was obviously dead.'

'No mistaking that limp feeling,' he agreed sagely. He was standing close to and a little behind me: I wondered whether this was standard procedure in such circumstances. If so, it made sense. After all, they didn't know me from Adam.

'Been in the Force long?' I asked, for something to say.

'Long enough. How d'you spell your name, sir? Two s's, two l's? And your home address?'

I told him. He looked musingly at the illuminated glass strip in the door. 'What brought you out this way tonight?'

'As a matter of fact,' I said readily, 'I'd had a phone call from —'

The door reopened, spilling more light over the footway. The senior officer, a lean-faced man of incongruously stocky build, emerged to take up a position on my other flank. Interrupting myself, I said, 'Did you find the weapon?'

He looked at me strangely for a moment. 'A weapon,' he repeated. 'No, I didn't. And what's more, I didn't find a body. There's nothing suspicious inside that kitchen that I can see.'

'He was under the worktop,' I insisted.

My voice echoed unconvincingly from the kitchen

walls. The two policemen looked sidelong at me, then at each other. Crouching, the senior man examined the floor beneath the worktop.

'No sign of anything.'

'That's where he was lying.' I heard my voice crack. 'There was blood all over the place.'

He felt the floor-tiles with a finger. 'Dry,' he commented. 'If someone mopped up, they did a thorough job with a clean rag.'

'You don't believe me, do you? You think I'm trying to be misleading. You're not prepared to—'

'Now don't get in a lather, Mr Cassell. We're as nonplussed as you are. How long since you first came in here and . . . saw your partner?'

'Half an hour, maybe.' I looked at my watch before stepping back into the living-room to check it against the clock. Constable Ward stepped adroitly with me. 'Nearer forty minutes,' I corrected myself. 'I ran a fair way to find a call box.'

The senior man joined us. 'Could have given 'em time,' he conjectured. 'Is there a back way out of here?'

'I've no idea.' I looked him straight in the eye. 'It's my first visit.'

After a pensive survey of the room he walked across to mount the two carpeted steps leading to the higher level. With a tug of a hanging cord he drew back the floor-length curtains, exposing latticed windows beyond which nothing could be seen in the darkness.

'All secured,' he remarked, 'from the inside.' Drawing the curtains, he swivelled. 'We've tested the bedroom windows. Jammed solid with paint. If your partner was carried out of here, Mr Cassell, he went through the street door. A mite risky, wouldn't you say? Anyone could have noticed.'

Constable Ward was looking around. 'Anywhere inside the apartment a body might be hidden?'

'Hardly a cupboard in sight,' said his superior. 'And I've looked under the bed.'

'Hidden cubbyholes?'

'Take another look,' said the senior man tolerantly, 'while I clarify a few more details with Mr Cassell.'

'I don't know how else I can help you.'

'My name's Sergeant Bradford,' he informed me, as though placing the whole matter on a new footing. 'It would be useful to know a little more about this partner of yours. His name's . . . Albert Hall, I believe you said. And this is where he lives, I take it?'

'No. He lives in Chelsea. I mean he did.'

'But this place must belong to him as well.'

'Why?'

He gave me a canny look. 'Well, he asked you here, apparently. You were telling Constable Ward you had a phone call . . .'

'Not from him.'

'Who, then?'

'An anonymous one. If I wanted to know where my partner was, why didn't I try this address? I forget the exact words.'

'Man or woman?'

I pretended to think about it. 'Disguised. Could have been either.'

'The call came out of the blue?'

'I had been wondering where my partner was. He'd been missing all day.'

'Ah. You'd reported his absence?'

'Not to the police. It seemed a bit soon to be kicking up a dust.'

'So then you got this call—what, an hour or two ago? And you came out here. Was the street door open when you arrived?'

'It was ajar. I rapped first but got no reply, so I shoved my way in.'

'Any lights burning?'

'No, the place was in blackness. I switched on a light and came in here. Nobody around, so I tried the kitchen. There he was, slumped on the floor under the worktop.'

'Did you touch him?'

'Just to check if he was dead.'

'You've seen a dead person before, Mr Cassell?'

'Er . . . no. But he *felt* dead. And there was the blood. There was no doubt in my mind.'

He withheld comment, but not for long. 'The assumption we tend to work on,' he said, watching the activities of the constable as he went about the apartment, 'is that human error must always be allowed for.'

'You're saying, I could have made a mistake?'

'You're maintaining you didn't?'

I lifted my shoulders. With a glance towards the bedroom, from which muffled thumps were emanating, he said briskly, 'Right. So we've got your business partner, Mr Albert Hall of Chelsea, missing for a day, then turning up apparently murdered on the kitchen floor of a Finchley apartment; and finally vanishing into thin air. Odd sequence of events. Did he have enemies?'

'None that I know of. Difficult to say, of course. His personal life wasn't an open book to me.'

'Married?'

'There's a wife, yes. I've called her a couple of times today, asking if she knew where he was. She didn't.'

'Wasn't she anxious to report him missing?'

'She's used to his absences.'

'I see,' he said in a colourless voice.

The constable reappeared. 'Blank so far,' he reported.

'Get outside, then, and shift the car. Mind stepping out with us, Mr Cassell? Time we made an enquiry or two, I think.'

Following him into the street, I decided I didn't much care for the set of his shoulders. They proclaimed scepticism. He was, I sensed, merely going through the motions of an investigation; humouring me, possibly. On one level, that was fine. I wasn't anxious to invite too many searching questions. On another, I wanted Albert's disappearance accounted for. At the end of a day of bizarre events, or non-events, this latest puzzle was threatening to send me over the top.

Sceptical or not, Sergeant Bradford did the commonsense thing and knocked at the door of the adjoining property to the right. Getting no response, he tried the one on the left, with the same result.

We moved on to the next door. A man in a zipped sweater and rimless spectacles presented himself after a protracted interval. He gave the impression that we had interrupted him in a study of silicon chip technology. Bradford handled him with care.

'Very sorry to disturb you, sir. I'm making a few enquiries about No. 31, two doors along. You don't happen to know the name of the occupier?'

Stepping on to the footway, the man gazed myopically along the street. 'Thirty-one?' He peeled off the spectacles. 'I might,' he said, continuing to gaze.

'Yes?' Bradford said hopefully.

'If somebody was in occupation.'

'You mean . . . ?'

'Laid empty for months. That place and the two either side.' The man indicated them with a jerk of the chin. 'Up for letting, they tell me. Probably get the blacks in.'

'Any idea who owns them, sir?'

The man shook his head and hissed. 'Some old bird. Used to, that is. Died, a year back. Can't say who has 'em now. Family, I dare say. Still debating what to do with 'em, if you ask me.'

Bradford said idly, 'People go in and out, I suppose, from time to time?'

'Couldn't say. We live at the back of the house — that's

my old mother and me. Don't see much of what goes on. Try the lot at No. 27. They might take more interest.'

Thanking him punctiliously, Bradford steered me away. Behind us, the door was firmly closed. Outside No. 31 Constable Ward stood waiting: he had found a parking space on the opposite side of the street. Bradford gestured me to wait there too. 'I'll just be a moment.'

We watched him storm the door of No. 27. After talking for several minutes to someone invisible to us inside, he returned with an expressionless face.

'Our other friend was right, it seems. These three are standing empty. There's reputedly some argument about what's to happen to them. For details of ownership we'd have to check with the agents, I imagine. As for today, no one seems to have noticed any undue activity hereabouts. But then, they all seem pretty wrapped up in their own affairs.'

Constable Ward looked sage. 'Sure to be one busybody along the street.'

'Why aren't they here, then, offering to help? We've created no interest whatever. No question, it's one of those streets of casual bedsitters and the like, where they all keep themselves to themselves.' Unexpectedly he turned to me. 'Any comment, Mr Cassell?'

'If these three properties are vacant,' I said slowly, 'why is No. 31 furnished? And how come the lights work?'

He shrugged. 'It may be on the point of getting a tenant.' He gazed up at the building with a frown. 'I can't quite get the hang of the layout. There's a floor above, as well. Is that a separate apartment? If so, how do you get to it?'

'From next door,' suggested Constable Ward, 'one side or the other.'

'Could the answer lie there?' I demanded suddenly.

They both looked at me.

Self-consciously I enlarged. 'If one of the neighbouring

doors gives access to that apartment overhead, couldn't my partner have been whisked through it and hidden up there while I was calling the police?'

They said nothing. I added, 'Or there might be a trapdoor in the ceiling of No. 31, connecting with the room above.'

'There isn't.' Bradford rested his spine against a parked van and folded his arms. 'And if there were, it would be quite an operation, heaving the body of a full-grown man from one floor to another via a hole in the ceiling. Or out of one door, into another and up the stairs, for that matter.'

Constable Ward made assenting noises. 'Unless it was a gang job.'

'Well, couldn't it have been?'

'Why would a gang want to fetch you out here, Mr Cassell, for a glimpse of the corpse on the kitchen floor, and then get rid of it?'

'As a warning, perhaps.'

Bradford looked alert. 'Have you been getting threats?'

'No, none. Of course, again, I can't speak for my partner.'

'What kind of business are you in?'

'Property conversions.'

He looked eloquently from me to the building, and back to me. I added dampeningly, 'We've always done everything on a joint basis. We've no interest in any properties in Finchley.'

'Mm. And, so far as you know, you've trodden on no toes recently? Had no occasion, for instance, to outbid or undercut a rival firm, in such a way as to threaten its livelihood?'

I shook my head with confidence. 'Absolutely not.'

He examined me with the impenetrable poker face of the eternal cop. 'Hard work, I imagine . . . property dealing?'

'It has its moments.'

'You're in a large way of business?'

'Moderately. But we don't run to a big staff.'

He nodded attentively. 'So the pressure can build up at times.'

It was my turn to look hard at him. 'Same as in any kind of work.'

'Looking back over, say, the past six months . . . would you describe them as having been exceptionally heavy, in a business sense?'

I turned on the pavement to confront him squarely. The stance of the constable stiffened: he moved slightly to his right, narrowing the gap between us.

'The drift of your remarks,' I told Bradford coldly, 'doesn't escape me. Why not come right out with it? I've been overworking and I'm having delusions. If that's what you think, we may as well have it out in the open where we can kick it around. Okay, you're entitled to your suspicions. It does look crazy, I admit.'

He didn't contradict me. He stood leaning against the van with the same expression of emotionless appraisal, and kept his own counsel.

'But I'm telling you. I saw my partner lying there on that kitchen floor. And if you grilled me for a week I wouldn't budge from that story. I *know* what I saw.'

Pushing himself away from the van's bodywork, he made a finger-signal to the constable. 'In that case,' he said resignedly, 'we'd better think about broadening the investigation a little.'

CHAPTER 9

The manner of the detective-sergeant was brusquer and, paradoxically, less unnerving than that of the uniformed pair.

His name, he informed me, was Johnson. Clearly he was a little tetchy at finding himself saddled with an extra case: I gathered he had been about to go off duty. Despite this, he applied himself to the task with a diligence I could only applaud. In return, I did my utmost to be helpful.

'I told Sergeant Bradford I couldn't guess at a motive. So, in the absence of any evidence, I can't blame him for doubting my word.'

'But you're still convinced you saw your partner's body lying there?'

'Utterly.'

'Notwithstanding that a search of all three of the vacant properties has turned up nothing?'

'Why should that affect my recollection?' I asked. 'I'm not drunk: I haven't been taking dope. My memory is quite distinct. He was there, and then he wasn't. That, to me, suggests one thing.'

'That he was carried outside to a vehicle and taken elsewhere?'

'Can you think of another explanation?'

'One or two,' he said tersely. 'But they can keep for a while. The immediate job is to establish that we do still have a missing person on our hands. If so, your story must obviously be taken seriously.'

'Thank you,' I said ironically. 'I did take the trouble, after all, to run half a mile to call the police. And I did go back to meet them. Does that imply a hoax?'

Pulling out a cigarette pack, he offered it and, when I declined, lit one for himself. A plume of smoke coiled into the space between us, clouding the atmosphere. It struck me as symbolic.

'You know,' he said, hooking a foot about a leg of his chair, 'If I were to tell you one twentieth of the tales spun to us in here at one time or another, you'd be incredulous. People every bit as lucid as yourself. Me, I don't surprise easily any more. I've less patience than I used to have, I grant that. On the other hand, I reckon I've a keener sense of smell. Nine times out of ten, I can sniff out a phoney. From you, Mr Cassell, I don't get a whiff of that kind.'

'Very grateful, I'm sure.'

'Don't crawl too early. We've a busy time ahead of us. Are you braced?'

'Eager,' I assured him. 'All I want is to get this cleared up.'

'Okay.' He jumped out of the chair. 'Let's get to it.'

While we were being driven by Constable Ward back towards central London, the flow of questions from Sergeant Johnson continued at a steady pace. Most of his enquiries related to the business transactions of Newstyle Properties. Like Sergeant Bradford, he was obviously struck by the fact that my declared discovery of Albert had occurred inside premises that were on the market for letting. I tried to make him understand that rentals formed no part of our operations.

'We're strictly a convert-and-sell outfit. Rent-collection doesn't interest us. You can forget that aspect.'

'Your partner,' he said obstinately, 'could have been chasing up some project of his own.'

'He'd have discussed it with me.'

'I've heard partners say that before.'

'Albert . . . Mr Hall was different. He really was. When it came to practical matters, he was first rate. Dealing with contractors and so forth. But he wouldn't have set up a scheme on his own initiative. He liked to be given the lead.'

Johnson twitched a shoulder. 'What's his wife like?'

'Medium height, slim build, fair . . .'

'I meant, what sort of a woman is she? Easy to get on with?'

'Very. Provided you're not married to her.'

He flipped me a glance from his side of the car. 'You're implying there's been trouble?'

'Probably no more than average.'

Johnson hawked mirthlessly. 'That says it all—and it says nothing. Put it this way. Were things bad enough for her to put out a contract on her old man?'

'Hire someone to kill him, you mean?' The shock I felt must have seeped into my voice. I saw him smile to himself.

'Maybe that's another thing you wouldn't credit, Mr Cassell. Sometimes it can take astoundingly little—or what seems so to the outsider—to drive a spouse to the ultimate solution.'

'A year in your job,' I said, 'and I think I'd want to shoot myself.'

'You didn't answer my question.'

'No, because I can't. How could anyone, except those directly concerned?'

He made a conceding gesture with both hands, and fell silent.

Chelsea Embankment was still active. Without instruction, the driver turned unhesitatingly into the driveway of Albert's apartment block: he seemed well acquainted with the area. Johnson was holding the rear door open before the car came to a stop at the entrance. More circumspectly, I joined him on the tarmac.

As we climbed the stairs I noticed that the driver was following us. I felt a certain grim amusement. Johnson, for all his protestations about my shining validity, was leaving nothing to chance. Well, that was his privilege. Place not your trust in mortals. You wouldn't believe this, Mr Cassell, but I'm still not one hundred per cent happy about you. Nothing personal, you understand. Purely this reservation I have, born of years of disillusioning experience . . . If this was how he felt, I couldn't condemn him. People who report the finding of corpses that subsequently dissolve can hardly expect to remain top of the police popularity poll.

As we reached the first-floor landing, he turned. 'Is she likely to be home?'

'She's out a good deal, I believe. I still think it might have saved trouble to have rung her first from the station.'

'In a case like this,' he said enigmatically, 'personal contact is to be preferred. Without prior consultation. This door here?'

He thumbed a 'Gong-gong' out of the bell-push. The uniformed driver waited soundlessly behind us. Glancing appreciatively around the carpeted landing, Johnson remarked, 'If this is the public bit, what are the apartments like? A man of taste, your partner. It hardly seems—'

A rattling of the door latch stopped him. He raised an eyebrow at me. 'Sounds like we're in luck.'

The door moved back.

'Steve!' exclaimed Albert. 'What brings you here, this time of night?'

Inside the apartment it was warm, and the seating was deep-sprung. Fatigue, physical and mental, pinned me to the cushions while I listened to their voices.

'According to your colleague here, Mr Hall, an hour or two ago you were lying on the floor of a house in Finchley. Unconscious or dead.'

'Finchley?' Albert repeated dazedly.

'Where we've just come from.' Johnson was speaking as though giving evidence in court. 'Mr Cassell reported finding you at around eight-thirty.'

Albert looked huntedly about him. 'What is all this, Steve? It doesn't—'

'I had this anonymous phone call.' It was myself talking. 'The voice mentioned this Finchley address and implied that you were there. So naturally I drove straight over.'

He blinked, shook his head like a surfacing bather. 'Why naturally? What made you think I might be there? Didn't you check here first?'

'Of course I did. You weren't here.'

'But I was. I've been indoors the whole evening.'

I waited a moment. 'Since what time?'

'Five thirty, quarter to six. Something like that. *Finchley*? I don't think I've set foot in the place for years.'

Johnson was watching us.

I said slowly and carefully, 'If you were at home from before six, you must have been under the shower or something when I called. I couldn't get a reply.'

Blankness sat on Albert's face. 'If I had been, which I wasn't, I can always hear the phone or the doorbell.'

'What about your wife, Mr Hall?' Johnson interposed. 'Was she here?'

'No. She was out when I got back. She plays bridge on Fridays.'

'Where?'

'I don't know where,' Albert said with restraint.

'But you yourself haven't moved from the apartment this evening?'

'I've barely got out of my chair. I was feeling a bit whacked after a hard day.'

'Where were you?' I demanded.

'Where was I? What do you mean?'

'We've been making enquiries about you all day.' I was no longer guarding my tongue. I was too angry. 'At one point I as good as reported you missing. Where the hell did you get to?'

There was no mistaking Albert's bewilderment; it rolled out of him like mist. He had to take an extra breath before he could reply.

'Reported me *missing*? What in God's name for?'

Rising from his chair, Sergeant Johnson stood looking down at the pair of us. 'This seems to need clarifying. You're saying, Mr Hall, there was no reason for your partner here to have been concerned at your absence from the office today?'

'Concerned? I can't . . .' Albert gibbered for a moment. 'He knew where I was. He *sent* me.'

'And where was that?' Johnson enquired, forestalling my question.

'Sevenoaks, to inspect a property we were interested in. Then on to Tonbridge, ditto, and back via Maidstone. It was all fixed up yesterday. You remember, Steve?'

I met his imploring glance with a stony face. Johnson continued to make the running. 'Was it a fruitful trip?'

'Not very. None of the properties was suitable for our purpose, as it happens.' Abandoning me in despair, Albert restored his attention to the sergeant. 'I didn't bother to phone Mr Cassell, because there was no urgency about it. I was going to report to him tomorrow. As for tonight, he knew I intended to come straight home.'

'I knew nothing of the sort. And neither did Amanda.'

'Amanda?' queried the detective.

'Our secretary,' Albert told him. 'She has everything at her fingertips. She must have known what my arrangements were.'

'Take my word for it,' I said, 'she was as much in the dark as I was. In fact, she spent half the day phoning round to the various sites, asking if anyone had seen you.'

'That's nonsense,' Albert said indignantly. 'I left a pile of letters yesterday for her to type, specifically because I was going to be out today. Of course she knew.'

'Ask her.'

'Gentlemen.' Johnson uplifted both arms, like the Pope blessing the multitude in St Peter's Square. 'We're tracking some way from the immediate points, which are to establish that you, Mr Hall, are neither dead nor missing;

and that you, Mr Cassell, have not been wilfully wasting police time. I think we can accept that Mr Hall is alive and well and living in Chelsea. On the second point, frankly, I'm less happy.'

'Don't understand it at all,' I heard Albert muttering.

I stood up. Tired though I was, fury was pumping adrenalin back into my limbs, and I preferred to confront Johnson on level terms. 'If you're not happy, perhaps you can imagine how I'm feeling. This entire thing is grotesque.'

'You can say that again—' from the sofa.

'Thanks, but I plan to say something more useful. You won't mind if I use your phone. What's Amanda's home number?'

'Now wait a bit.' Johnson checked my progress across the room. 'I'm conducting this enquiry, Mr Cassell. If we're going to verify statements, we'll do it properly. Where does your secretary live?'

'Putney,' volunteered Albert. 'Park Terrace.'

'That's not far.' Johnson consulted his driver, statuesque by the door. 'Ten, fifteen minutes? We'll go and see her. Not all of us,' he added, as Albert made uncoiling movements. 'No need for you to turn out, Mr Hall, since you've had a strenuous day.' If the remark had an edge, it was not sharpened by his tone. 'Your partner can come with me. We'll be in touch with you again afterwards. Constable Ward will keep you company till we get back.'

'I don't need company,' Albert protested. 'I'm not in fear of anything.'

Johnson gave him a slight smile. 'I am, though,' he said gently. 'Just a little.'

Back inside the car, he clipped his seat belt and waited for me to do the same before engaging gear and moving us off. 'I hope,' he remarked, looking both ways several times before venturing into the main road, 'this isn't going to spell the ruination of a good partnership.'

I remained silent.

'Or am I assuming too much? Has trouble been building up between the two of you?'

'Up until today,' I said thickly, 'we couldn't have combined better. I don't understand it . . . I never shall. My partner, as well as being a personal friend—'

'My advice to you, Mr Cassell, is to hold your horses for the moment. That's what I'm doing. You realize something? You could both be making a monkey out of me.'

'What possible motive—'

'I had a case once,' he said reminiscently, 'in which three separate people, over a two-day period, reported seeing a naked woman riding a donkey through a local park and trampling the rose-beds. We took it seriously, interviewed the head keeper, posted spies, the works. Never a sight of this latter-day Godiva. So we grilled the three again. You know what? They'd had a bet with their pub pals: if they could con the cops for longer than a week, they were on fifty quid apiece. Now, I'm not saying this is anything along those lines . . .'

'Neither Mr Hall nor I,' I said tightly, 'have got time to organize idiotic wagers.'

Johnson inclined his head. 'I'm ready to believe that. As I say, I'm keeping an open mind.'

With some help from me, he found his way to Amanda's street with only a couple of minor delays. As he braked outside her buff brick 1970s maisonette, I said, 'Do you want to see her by yourself? Her name's Miss Barnes.'

'She'll be less thrown if you're with me. But let me do the talking, if you don't mind.'

At his ring, the lobby light flashed on instantly. We then had a view of Amanda's legs, from the knees downwards, descending the open plan stairs. Spotting us through the all-glass door, she paused doubtfully before recognizing me, smiling widely and hurrying the rest of the way to release the catch. She looked comfortable in a sweater and loose skirt.

'What a surprise!' She glanced curiously from me to the sergeant. 'Won't you come in?'

It occurred to me, as we responded, that our unannounced arrival was a bonus event, pennies from heaven that she was going to make the most of. Shutting the door, she looked at us expectantly. I said, 'Sorry to drop in on you like this, Amanda. There's no problem. This is, um, Detective-Sergeant Johnson, who thinks you might be able to help on a small matter. D'you mind?'

The animation died out of her face. 'Of course not,' she said faintly. 'Is it something I've —'

Johnson said quickly, 'Nothing directly to do with you, Miss Barnes. You can rest easy. It's just that you're probably in a position to clear up a minor mystery, if you'll be so kind.'

'Oh.' She gave a small gulp. 'Would you like to come up?'

Her eyes met mine as she turned, and I slipped her a rallying grin. The effort was prodigious, but I managed.

The first-floor living-room was tricked out as a kind of studio/conservatory. Potted plants were everywhere, trailing foliage over shelving and furniture. Where there were no tendrils there was a newspaper, a magazine or a travel brochure. Trampling through it all, we positioned ourselves in a triangular group near the window. Amanda looked up into Johnson's face.

'What I'm after,' he said crisply, 'is an outline of today's routine at the office.'

'An outline . . . ?'

'I'd like to know what happened while you were there.'

Her nose wrinkled. 'I don't know that anything *happened*. It was just an ordinary sort of day. What do you want to find out, in particular?'

I made a movement which Johnson smoothly covered.

'Just tell me, in a few words, what you did yourself.'

'Well . . . Typed some letters. Opened the mail. Took a few calls.' She gave me a mystified glance. 'There's not much else to say.'

Johnson eyed her gravely. 'Did you *make* any calls?'

'I made one to a friend, cancelling an engagement tomorrow. Oh, and a quick one to the Frimley Street College, about my class this evening. I'm taking a first-aid course,' she explained shyly, as Johnson waited. 'I had an exam tonight. I haven't long been back, actually.'

'You made no other calls?'

Uneasily she shook her head. 'Was I supposed to have done?'

I couldn't contain myself. 'You're forgetting a few, aren't you, Amanda?'

Johnson let it ride. She regarded me intently, in a transparent attempt to say the right thing. 'Am I? It's quite likely. I do things in a dream, sometimes.' She smiled hopefully at the detective.

'Did you at any time make a series of calls on behalf of Mr Cassell?'

'What about?'

'Concerning his partner, Mr Hall.'

Again the headshake, hesitant but unstoppable. 'No. I'm quite sure I didn't do that.'

'Amanda . . . think carefully. Just after you came back from lunch. Remember?'

'I really can't,' she said miserably. 'What did it have to do with Mr Hall?'

While I was staring at her, Johnson took over again. 'Mr Cassell tells us you phoned around the company's sites to try and locate Mr Hall, who hadn't shown up at the office. Is that right?'

Amanda's eyes were wide and glazed. 'He'd gone to Sevenoaks,' she said, almost in a whisper. 'We knew we couldn't get hold of him.'

'So you didn't make those calls?'

'No—why should I? There wouldn't have been any point.'

'Mr Cassell maintains he asked you to. He says he was very worried at Mr Hall's non-appearance and wanted to find out where he was.'

Amanda was no longer looking my way. She was focusing exclusively upon the sergeant, as though hopeful of bringing about his physical dissolution by means of one more straight answer.

'I think you must have misunderstood him. He couldn't have been worried, because he knew Mr Hall was travelling down to Sevenoaks to look at a property. In fact, he remarked on it as he came into the office. 'We've a quiet day ahead'—that's what he said. 'Bob in South London and Mr Hall doing the grand tour of Kent.' That's Bob Callis, our surveyor. He spent the day at Greenwich. So you see, Mr Cassell couldn't have asked me to phone around. He'd have known it was pointless.'

Silence clamped down on the room.

After a few moments I tried to loosen its grip. 'She's got things muddled, you know. She's thinking of some other day.'

Johnson nodded, not in assent. 'Or somebody is.'

I walked away, sending a potted begonia to the floor with my elbow. In the centre of the room I spun round.

'To hell with it!' I shouted. 'What's the matter with you, Amanda? Have you gone stark raving mad?'

She burst into tears. 'I don't know how you wanted me to answer,' she wailed. 'What did you want me to say?'

CHAPTER 10

Waiting beside the car, I gazed numbly at the illuminated lobby of the maisonette. I seemed to be making something of a habit of standing in streets after dark, staring at habitations. The distinctions were starting to blur. Which one was this? I had to think hard, simply to remember where I was and why. And when I succeeded, the effort had got me nowhere.

Johnson came out. As he regained the pavement, the lobby light was extinguished, leaving the curtained light upstairs as the only hint of occupation. Amanda, I thought, would be busy with brush and pan, painstakingly repotting the begonia, removing earth from the carpet. I felt sorry to have caused a mess.

'Shall we be away?' asked the sergeant.

I sat looking ahead. Beside me, he concentrated on the controls and other road-users, keeping his own counsel. The atmosphere became unbearable.

'Either she's suffered a brainstorm or I have. And I don't think it's me.'

Johnson offered no comment.

'Do I look or sound like someone experiencing fantasies? Chronic delusion?' I turned my head. 'Would you mind explaining something to me? Will you tell me what fulfilment you think I'm getting out of making a damn fool of myself?'

He said pensively, 'What sort of physical health do you enjoy, Mr Cassell?'

'Very sound, thanks.'

'But you're registered with a doctor, I assume?'

'Most people are.'

'That doesn't answer the question.'

'Now you know the feeling.'

'You're in no position to try backchat with me, Mr Cassell.' His tone didn't alter, but the words reduced me to dumbness. 'I'm being very patient. As patient as I know how. I happen to think you were just as disconcerted by that interview back there as Miss Barnes was. It's only an opinion, mind. I could be wrong. So don't push your luck.'

'I wasn't meaning to be obstructive.' I spoke humbly. 'You must see I'm totally confused. I'm trying to steer back on course, but it's not easy. What was it you were asking?'

'Doctor.'

'I'm on the books of a very good man: Shilton. He's got a practice in the City.' I paused. 'You're suggesting that tomorrow might be a rather good day for a consultation?'

'It's a thought.'

He took the car up to the entrance to Albert's apartment block. I waited again while he vanished inside, to reappear shortly with Constable Ward, who took up his former position behind the wheel. Johnson motioned me to join him at the back. When we were moving again, he produced a pad and ballpen and began to make notes.

'Contrary to what you may be imagining,' I said quietly, 'I have not, repeat not, been overworking. Things have actually been rather quiet. I enjoy my work. It's what I thrive on. During my slacker times, I play squash and I swim at a private and very expensive club in Granville Place. I tend not to fret. I never bottle things up. I have a good, relaxed existence.'

He went on scribbling.

'There are no cash problems. Newstyle Properties makes a trading profit. My emotional life is fine. I don't have a history of mental disease. Neither does anyone in my family. I don't lie sleepless at nights, agonizing over world affairs. I don't pop pills. The last time I attended

Dr Shilton's surgery, four years ago, he gave me a penicillin jab for a poisoned finger. If there's such a thing as a contented human being, that's what I am. Was.'

Pocketing the notepad, Johnson sat back, folded his arms. 'On the face of it, you're something of a phenomenon.'

'Just nicely normal.'

'I'd still make an appointment with that quack of yours.'

'He's not a psychiatrist,' I said steadily.

'But he could offer an opinion—'

'Are you seriously telling me I should go and ask him whether I'm crackers?'

'Purely in your own interests, Mr Cassell.'

'And if I refuse . . . purely in my own interests?'

'Nobody can force you to do anything,' he said calmly. 'On the other hand, I could make things . . . inconvenient for you. You've taken up a lot of police hours this evening.'

'I do apologize. I was under the absurd impression that the police existed to investigate abnormal occurrences. Stupid of me.'

'No need for sarcasm.'

'It's about all I can summon up just now. Put yourself in my place. Suppose you went back to your HQ tonight and said you'd been out on a case, and everyone wagged their heads and said, Oh no, you've been here all the time, sitting at that desk writing out a report, don't you remember? How would you react to that?'

'I never speculate. The plain fact is, Mr Cassell, you're the bloke currently on the receiving end, I'm afraid.' His tone moderated. 'I'm not sniping. You're in a flat spin, I can see that, and I sympathize. This is why I mentioned the doctor. He might be able to put his finger on something. It's what he's there for. Why not give it a whirl?'

With an assumption of submissiveness I settled back.

'It's a deal,' I said wearily. 'I'll go first thing after the weekend.'

'Good.'

Presently I added, 'What else did Amanda tell you after I left?'

'The same, in rather more detail. Having described the office routine, she gave me chapter and verse on your arrangement with your partner whereby he was to spend the day out of town. There's no question about it. That was the understanding.'

I gesticulated feebly. 'I don't want to think about it any more. Not tonight.'

'Sensible decision. Take my advice again—get a night's sleep and come back to it fresh, in daylight. The picture may be sharper. I'll have to be in touch with you again tomorrow, or somebody will. But don't worry about it. It's for your own benefit as much as ours.'

'Spare me the avuncular touch.'

'I don't blame you for being prickly,' he said. 'But don't build up too much of a thing about the police, will you? One of these days, you might really need us.'

After they had dropped me off, I stood watching the car's tail-lamps until they vanished at the intersection. Then I trudged across to the block entrance and entered the building.

It was the performance of this manœuvre that reminded me of my car.

Unless, like Albert's, it had been towed away, it was still parked in a lay-by outside a newsagent's in Finchley. I had forgotten it entirely. Nobody had enquired how I had got to Finchley in the first place, and in my half-stunned condition I had submitted passively to being ferried around in police transport; so in a sense the oversight was understandable. Now here I was, physically as well as mentally stranded. The knowledge that no metal hunk of mobility awaited me in the garage below was, in the circumstances, doubly disturbing. Yet another prop had been deftly kicked away from under me.

It didn't really matter. I could pick it up in the morning. My sense of isolation could hardly be greater.

Or so I thought, until I entered the lift. Like many people, I have never doted on lifts. They are one of the necessary but deplorable drawbacks of apartment life. Those serving my block were unnervingly efficient, operating in virtual silence, with the occasional distant sigh the sole audible notification of progress up or down or to a standstill. I had never been sorry to step out of them.

This evening, the trip to the fifth floor seemed to take three times as long as usual. In the vastness of my relief when the floor under my soles did cease vibrating and the door slid open, I all but leapt into the corridor, mindless of fatigue or possible impediment: the shock of the ensuing collision was all the greater as a consequence. In the dim corridor lighting, the arms clutching me belonged to an impalpable figure. The voice, however, was unmistakable, although it was pitched on a hiss.

'Come on, Steve. Make it snappy.'

'What the—'

'Save your breath. Let's get along to your apartment. We don't want to attract notice.'

'You've got a bloody—'

'Come *on*, you cretin. Got your door key handy?'

Something in the way he spoke set me searching my pocket as he hurried me along. Once we were inside the lobby he relaxed, sagging back against the door to run over me a quizzical survey that, in the purest sense, was alien to all that I had ever associated with the Alberts of this planet. He seemed, if the apparent contradiction can be accepted, nervy but assured; like a thoroughbred racehorse awaiting the off.

'Saw them drop you outside,' he said, puffing his cheeks. 'Kept you talking a bit, didn't they? Gave me time to get up here ahead of you. What were they doing, telling you where to report in the morning?'

'Are you interested?' I could think of nothing else to say. I saw now why I had failed immediately to recognize him in the corridor. He was clad in a green anorak with a hood which gave a different shape to his face. The outfit was light years from his normal attire of dark suit and gleaming white shirt.

'Sorry if I startled you,' he said laconically. 'I had to improvise. The moment you'd all left my place, I jumped into the car and followed you over here.'

'How did you know they'd bring me home? I could have spent the night being questioned at the nick.'

'In the first place,' he said, shaking his head, 'they told me they were taking you home. In the second, I reckoned they must have asked all the questions they had up their sleeve for the moment. Looks like I was right, doesn't it?' He studied me, his mouth showing a tendency to quiver. 'Did they recommend medical treatment?'

'Since you mention it, that's precisely what was suggested. Maybe I can't blame them, but you're something else. What's going on? Are you round the twist or am I?'

'I'll explain later. Anything you want to pick up?'

'Pick up? What are you talking about?'

'Before we leave,' he said impatiently.

'I'm not going anywhere.'

'You have to, Steve. No time to explain now, but believe me it's vital. To both of us. Trust me, will you?'

'My faith in you, Albert, isn't quite what it was, I have to confess.'

'I'm sorry about what happened back there.' Zipping the anorak to his throat, he checked in the lobby mirror that the hood was in place. 'I'd no way of preparing you, so of course you were hit for six. No wonder that detective-sergeant got the wrong idea. He's seeing you again, I suppose?'

'Monday,' I said grimly. 'After I've seen the doctor.'

'Well, don't give it a thought. Long before then, everything should be straightened out. If you're not bringing anything, let's go, shall we?'

'Hey—where to? If it's back to that blasted dump in Finchley—'

'It's not,' he said swiftly. 'But we may have to go that way initially. Did you leave your car around there?'

'Yes, outside a shop. I was going back for it in the morning.'

'We'll fetch it now.' Placing finger and thumb on the door catch, he looked back at me narrowly, like Carruthers of the Foreign Office; I wondered why, far from wanting to laugh, I felt instead an obscure excitement. 'I don't want to be theatrical,' he said, 'but I'll slip away first, I think. Give me a couple of minutes, then follow. It's unlikely, but your buddy Sergeant Johnson could have taken it into his head to double back and infiltrate the building on the off-chance. No sense in playing into his hands.'

'Where will you be?'

'Take the stairs, not the lift. Meet me down in the garage. There's a pedestrian exit from there to the back of the building, right? That's where I'm parked.' Opening the door a cautious inch, he squinted into the corridor, then glanced back. 'See you below,' he whispered, and slipped out.

Dizzily I went through to the kitchen. Hacking an inch or two from a loaf, I added a wedge of cheese and some butter and dropped it all into a polythene bag, cramming the package into a pocket of my overcoat. The other pocket accommodated a small flask of whisky and water. There was no time to do more. Switching off the light, I returned to the lobby; then went back and switched the light on again. After that I left the apartment.

Albert was waiting in a far corner of the garage, near the exit sign. 'See anybody?' he asked.

'Not a soul.'

'Come on, then.' He led the way up a concrete staircase to the street, which yet again was being battered by cold rain. Within an asphalted rectangle beneath pillars at the rear of the building, a dozen or so vehicles were berthed for the night. Albert's Lancia stood at the end of the line, overshooting the painted markings but causing no obstruction. The interior was still warm. Backing out adroitly, he scanned the street with care before gliding the car away, using a tenth of its performance. 'That,' he said on a key of satisfaction, 'is passably that.'

'Any chance of an explanation now?'

'Have patience. For the moment I want to concentrate.' Hooded as he was, in the gloom he looked like an emaciated Friar Tuck at the wheel. Presently he added, 'Apologies once more, old chap. I appreciate how you must be feeling.'

'You can't imagine the half of it.' I glanced at him curiously as he drove. 'Apart from everything else, I'm wondering if I ever knew you, Albo. You're like a different person.'

A chuckle came out of him. 'You know what they say, Steve. We all have our other sides. What you're seeing right now is mine.'

We purred through Moorgate, headed for Islington. He was keeping, I saw, a firm check on the following traffic, allowing most of it to overtake. After a mile or two it was obvious that nothing was on our tail. Resettling himself, he released some breath.

'End of Reel Five,' he observed. 'Now for the climax.'

Bringing out the flask, I took a swig and put it back. It did nothing for my brain cells.

'This has been the damnedest forty-eight hours of my

life. I can't seem to catch up. Without wanting to seem clamorous, I'd be glad if you'd tell me one thing. Was Amanda following instructions?'

'A good secretary,' he said cryptically, 'always acts in her employer's best interests.'

'I'm not sure what that's supposed to mean, but she was damn convincing.'

'Amanda's a bright girl.'

'I wonder sometimes,' I said thoughtfully, 'whether she has much of a life outside the office. She attends evening classes, I know, for this and that. But I've never heard her mention a boy-friend. Have you?'

Albert changed gear for a bend. He was driving with great care. 'She was let down, some while back.'

'Oh?'

'I don't mean jilted. It never reached that stage. She had one of those hopeless longings for someone who didn't react.'

'That's tough. How come you know about it?'

Albert looked a little shifty. 'I was going through a sticky patch myself at the time. The one I'm still negotiating.' I saw him swallow. 'You know how it is. She let something slip, I came back with something else . . . we sort of developed an understanding, and I think we helped each other over a bad period.'

It sounded maudlin. But it tended to confirm what I had half guessed: the relationship between Albert and Amanda had, for a while at least, outpaced the superficial business one, although how far they had taken it was anybody's guess. In the normal way I wouldn't have been concerned. Albert's private life was his own, and as long as Amanda's work didn't suffer—which it hadn't—she could operate as she liked on the emotional level without causing me a moment's disturbance.

'Interesting,' I remarked. 'But it doesn't tell me any more about this current rigmarole.'

'Patience, Steve.'

I flipped a hand in disgust. 'Okay. While I'm being patient, you don't mind if I wolf a hunk of bread and Stilton? I'm famished.'

'So long as you don't offer me any.'

While I ate, we motored docilely through Camden Town and Chalk Farm, to Belsize Park, from where Albert eased the car westwards into the Finchley area. Navigating deftly, he found his way to the road in which stood the premises of J. Barnsley, Newsagent and Confectioner. My car was where I had left it, parked with its nearside front tyre crushed painfully into the kerbstone. Instead of stopping, Albert drove on to the crest of the hill before pulling into a bus bay and leaning across me to open the door.

'Tidy step back,' he apologized, 'but I didn't want to put up signals. I'll wait here while you collect.'

'Then what?'

'I want you to tuck in behind me and stay there. Just keep following. I shan't drive fast.'

'Where are we going?'

'All part of the ultimate clarification package,' he said with a faint smile. 'It's a good forty-minute drive, that I can tell you. Feel braced after your snack?'

'Some coffee would help.'

'We'll see,' he said, like some semi-indulgent parent. 'Stay close, now.'

I walked back downhill through the rain. Crossing the mouth of the junction, I peered nervously along the street containing the enigmatic No. 31, but I could see no trace of activity of any kind. The police car seemed to have gone. Nobody was about. Nobody except me, plodding through the downpour in the darkness.

Albert's explanation, I thought, had better be good. He owed me a couple of nights' sleep.

Unlocking the car door, I slid inside and tried the

starter. For an unpleasant few moments it whirred vainly: I had visions of drenched leads that would need drying out. Then it kicked, and the stroke after that it fired. Turning in the road, I headed for Albert's waiting tail-lamps.

CHAPTER 11

I wasn't sorry when we peeled off the motorway.

On a fine night, keeping the Lancia within view would have been no problem. In an embracing mist of descending rain and ascending spray, with rival traffic dodging between us, and gale-force gusts swooping down from the embankments, it came at times close to impossibility. Only Albert's promised sedateness of pace enabled me to stay in contact. At one stage the Lancia slowed drastically, dropping back to within a few yards of me, and as it did so its nearside indicator winked me into a turnoff lane. I pursued it to the top of the rise, where it fed us into a minor road leading away to the west. Forest land on both sides shielded it from the worst of the storm, and the Lancia picked up speed.

By now I was nearly dropping with fatigue. The bread and cheese and whisky had patched me up for a while, but I needed a square meal, a long leisurely drink . . . and nine hours' uninterrupted slumber. One thing kept me going. Inside an hour or two, Albert had promised, I should receive a coherent explanation of recent events. For that, I was willing to put up with any amount of temporary inconvenience.

In my anxiety not to lose him, I had taken no note of direction signs or nameplates. At a guess, we had left the motorway somewhere south of Dunstable and were now heading into Buckinghamshire. The road that was taking us along was less than minor; it had barely outgrown infancy. Signposts, apparently, were alien to its structure. No other road deemed it worth crossing. The layabout gang who had built it hadn't bothered too much with drainage, either. Cataracts of water kept sloshing the windscreen, to be got rid of by the wipers in readiness for the next volley. Repeatedly, the car's nearside wheels bounced into ruts, squeezing mildly expostulatory grunts from the suspension.

It was all right, I thought sourly, for the Lancia with its ultra-broad tyres, its spoilers and dampers. My Ford, from the middle range, had no cross-country pedigree that I knew of, and although eager to please it had its limitations. I hoped nothing snapped or flooded. Conditions weren't ideal for a repair job.

Forty minutes, Albert had said. Since leaving Finchley, we had now been driving for well over an hour. No doubt his estimate had been based on a dry run. Either that, or he was hopelessly lost.

Ordinarily, this was the first possibility that would have occurred to me. It was a measure of his sudden rise in my esteem that I was still prepared, at this stage, to grant him the benefit of the doubt.

I was on the point of flashing my headlamps at him, in the hope of inducing a halt for consultation, when the road broadened and the surface improved. A whiff of familiarity brushed against me.

I had been here before. Half a dozen times, but from the opposite direction, from Aylesbury. To my left, a sign loomed; then a stone-pillared entrance, confirming the realization. I knew this place.

Driving between the gateless pillars, Albert set a modest pace along the narrow metalled track across parkland. I knew it was parkland although I couldn't see it. In the past few months the land could not have changed much, even if the house had. And outwardly, I knew, the house itself would be much the same. Inside: that was where Newstyle Properties was making its presence felt.

With a tangible objective so close, I began to feel lighter in spirits. But also puzzled.

What did eighteenth-century Pendover Manor have to do with the riddle?

After a third of a mile the track became a drive; two hundred yards later, a gravelled expanse in front of the columned façade. Again, the bulk of the building was merely an outline against the night sky, silhouetted by the radiance from our headlamps; but I could recall enough of its detail for a picture to form in my mind. A stepped approach to a porticoed entrance in the centre of the building, a stylishly symmetrical affair of brick and stone, with a flat roof encircled by a balustrade. The first time Albert and I had set eyes upon Pendover Manor, we had seen the possibilities. The interior was a wreck. During the war, troops had been billeted there for some unguessable purpose, and after their departure no one had admitted responsibility for the place for thirty years. But in a sense the War Department had been right. It was made for multiple occupation.

The difference between their approach and ours was purely one of motivation. They had wanted it to shelter as many heads as possible, at minimum expense, for a limited term. We wanted to spend, and were spending, more than a quarter of a million pounds to give a dozen or so potential residents the best of two worlds. *Stately seclusion in glorious countryside . . . luxury apartments within easy reach of nearby towns . . . ready access by road and rail to London.* Our printed literature said it all.

As far as I knew, work on the project had been progressing to plan. If there had been constructional snags, Albert hadn't seen fit to mention them. Preoccupied with other schemes, I had left the supervision of this one largely to him during the past three months. Had something gone badly wrong?

Parking behind him at the foot of the steps, I kept the headlamps on and struggled out apprehensively into the gale. He joined me on the gravel. His wet hair was blowing comically over his eyes. I shielded my own against the thrashing rain.

'What's the trouble?' I bawled. 'Why did we have to come out here in the middle of the night?'

He said nothing, but showed me, significantly, a key in his right hand. With an acquiescent shrug I returned to my car and doused the lights; he did the same, and we met up again on the steps. At the top, I stood back while he unfastened the weighty oak door, stepped through and switched on the porch light. Following, I reclosed the door, blocking out the weather noise as though I had slammed down a ship's hatch.

When I turned, Albert had the inner doors open and more lights on. I tailed him through to the vaulted entrance hall, avoiding the stacks of timber and plasterboard that claimed much of the floorspace. Our feet rang on boards, many of them recently replaced. Although the atmosphere was chill, there was no hint of mustiness. A combined scent of paint and sawdust predominated.

I gazed around. 'They seem to be doing a good job. How come the lights are working?'

'They hitched up to the private supply,' Albert explained.

The Manor boasted its own generator, powered by a stream that flowed through the grounds. 'Wiring's all finished, then?' I asked.

He nodded. 'They fixed that up first, so that work could go on after dark. Good bunch, Thompson's. Nice to deal with. I was thinking we might use them again, if another property crops up around these parts. Shall we take a look at what they've done?'

I turned to gaze at him.

'Albo,' I said, 'I'm extremely interested, as you know, in progress on all our undertakings. I like to see what's going on. But you didn't bring me out here on a wild night in March to have a look at the decorations?'

He looked hurt. 'It's rather more than a paint-and-paper job. They've virtually had to gut the inside and start afresh.'

'I know that,' I said patiently. 'I'm the guy who worked most of it out, remember? And it's great to see it materializing. I'd intended paying another visit soon, anyhow. But frankly, I wasn't planning on making it tonight. I do have other things on my mind.' I paused. 'And so do you, I thought.'

Again he nodded, more decisively.

'Sorry, Steve. I do want to explain, but first I thought we might take a look at the show flat. Cosier in there.'

'Is it finished?'

'Pretty well.' He pointed to our right. 'We made it that one. Easily accessible, so anyone inspecting it won't interfere with work elsewhere. Come and see what you think.'

The outer door to the show flat had been stripped and sanded ready for varnishing. While Albert was unlocking it, I observed that most of the other woodwork in the entrance hall had yet to be similarly prepared, and guessed that work on the remaining six apartments was less advanced. Three of the total seven were at ground level, and four overhead. The doors to these could be seen along the gallery that ran around three sides of the hall.

'I think it's going to work,' I said.

'Let's hope so.' He waved me through.

'Maybe we can find another like it.'

'No luck yet . . . but I'm still looking.' He gestured around the inner lobby, which was about the size and height of a small theatre. 'Not a bad first impression to dazzle your guests with, huh? I wasn't sure about the decor, but I think it comes off. This is nothing, though. Wait till you see—' he threw open another door—'the main reception area. How about that?'

I stood in appreciative silence while he flicked on more lights. Formerly a library, the room had been skilfully transformed with the aid of modern touches that avoided interference with the period flavour, giving it the functional allure of a five-star hotel suite coupled with the elegance of an eighteenth-century drawing-room. Armchairs and sofas upholstered in deep red wallowed in royal-blue carpeting that stretched away like the Pacific to lap at the shores of full-width bookshelves on each side of the magnificent fireplace at the far end. The walls were oak-panelled. The ceiling decorations had been lovingly restored.

I said, 'I like it.'

'Yours for a hundred and forty thousand. Leasehold.'

'I thought we fixed on one-fifty?'

'Whatever.' He ran a critical finger down the grain of a panel.

'How about the bedrooms?' I asked.

'Take a look, while I see about that coffee I half-mentioned. You know where the kitchen is? Out to the lobby again, turn left.'

When I rejoined him he was measuring instant coffee granules into a couple of china mugs on a working surface beneath a curved window masked by blinds. 'Sorry about the receptacles,' he remarked, recapping the coffee jar and sliding it away. 'Hardly a match for the furniture and fittings. Now that you've seen the place, what do you think?'

'I still think we're on to a winner.'

'So do I. Once we sell three, we break even. The rest is profit.'

'Think they'll sell?'

'Butterfield tells me they've had several enquiries

already.' Having poured scalding water on to the granules, Albert punched a hole in a tin of evaporated milk, added a little to each mug and handed me one. 'Sugar.' He indicated a split bag. 'The ultimate in gracious living. Yes, Steve, I'm pretty optimistic. In my considered judgement, Newstyle Properties can't lose over this.'

I hadn't seen or heard him so cheerful for months. After a few sips of his very strong coffee I rested the mug. 'For someone who's been through a traumatic experience, you seem in remarkably good form.'

'It's all this talk of monetary gain.'

'There must be some other factor,' I argued. 'Last night and the night before were a knockout for both of us. Something's changed—am I right?'

He reflected. 'Developed. Drink your coffee and I'll tell you about it.'

Sitting on a padded stool at the breakfast bar, I added more sugar to the mug and swallowed some more of the mixture. Lack of proper nourishment and rest was sneaking up on me again. My knees felt weak; my head was poising itself for a tentative pirouette. 'You owe me an explanation,' I confirmed. It was all I could do to muster an interest.

'Three minutes,' he promised. 'I just have to go to the bathroom.'

In his absence I swilled the rest of the coffee down the sink. The action entailed climbing off the stool and covering a yard of distance; I wondered why it took me so long and why, once there, I was seized with the ambition to shirk the return trip. The stool, after all, was at least a support. The sink was uncomfortable to lean against, and yet it held me as though magnetized. Feebly I tried to push it off. My arms had all the strength and spring of macaroni.

A door clashed. Footfalls thudded. Dimly I was aware

of Albert's return through the kitchen door. 'Said you'd explain,' I reminded him, slurring the syllables across the phrase like treacle over turf. 'Patient up to now. But it's time . . . time . . .'

I stopped for breath. The mere effort of opening my mouth was becoming difficult. Speech was next to impossible. It seemed to be taking more from my chest than I could replace: I heard myself panting. Albert was regarding me curiously. I made a supreme bid.

'. . . to level with me. You did promise.' The final word expired on a gasp.

'Quite right,' said Albert.

The two words rolled about the kitchen. One of them bowled straight at me along the worktop: seeing it coming, I tried to duck. The light went out. I could hear but not see. 'Right . . . right . . . right . . . right-right-right-right-right . . .' Spreadeagled, I whirled downwards.

Poe had it wrong. Flap both arms and you could delay your descent into the Maelstrom. But not interminably. For a while you could drift, rotating. Then you took a header, and dived and dived.

Someone had left the light on.

From the ceiling, it burned unwinkingly. A waste of energy. Squandering of the earth's resources. I didn't need it: I wanted to sleep. By a change of posture I could shield my eyes from the glare. Just by turning over.

I tried.

Presently I stopped trying. The exertion was getting me nowhere, except into hazy realms of pain. The discomfort seemed to be concentrated at my elbows, knees and ankles, as though the bone and sinew had knitted solid while I dreamt. I remembered dreaming. The detail was clouded.

Perhaps by shutting my eyes . . .

Inside my head there was pain of a separate quality. A

pulsing torment, as if my skull had been an old-fashioned hooter control between the undiscriminating fingers of a teenage driver. Squeeze . . . release . . . squeeze . . . No mercy. An endless route, headlong motion, the incessant tightening of the fingers. Stop the journey.

The light continued to burn. As well as being above, it was a little way ahead of me: it seemed to have competition. By lowering my gaze I could see an oblong of translucence, orange-tinted, facing me from a distance of a few yards. In some way, the oblong was at odds with the bulb.

I struggled to work out the discrepancy.

What troubled me most of all was the silence, the quite extraordinary stillness that engulfed me. When I stirred, I could hear the grinding of joints inside my own body. There was no faint sound of traffic, no distant clash of doors: the quiet was total.

It made it hard to think.

But eventually I hit on the connection. Or lack of one. The translucence was daylight behind an orange blind. Therefore the activated bulb was doubly superfluous. If someone were to pull up the blind, natural light would spill through and the artificial kind could be dispensed with.

There was no reason why I shouldn't do it myself. No reason, except that I couldn't move.

Once this fact was clear in my mind, panic started to seep in.

I fought it. I brought up the guns I had deployed as a lad, sweating and terrified in the black well of my bedroom, menaced by goblins, precluded from an appeal to indifferent adulthood by the greater fear of ridicule. 'I *know* there is nothing there . . .' reiterated soundlessly a thousand times, a barricade against invasion. 'I can't move—so what?' The words escaped in a mumble, unblocking the crucial valve. Before long I was calmer, partially in control. If I kept still, it was not too bad. Essential to remain still.

The twine securing me had been employed in multiple strands, doubled and redoubled in such a way as to prevent flexing. I was tied at ankles, knees and forearms, down to the fingertips: in addition I was bonded to something hard, immovable. Although my spine was clamped against it, I managed to twist my neck sufficiently to get a sight of a section of the fixture. It was the cooker.

The twine, I deduced, ran right round it and was knotted at the back or side. Trussed as I was, I could have gone straight into the oven and been roasted to a turn.

At least I wasn't gagged. I took breath into my lungs. 'Albert!'

In the ceramic confines of the kitchen, the echoes came back at me like a fusillade of tennis balls from a practice net. Something was creating resonance: the stainless steel double-sink unit, perhaps, facing me from the far side of the floor-tiles. The urge to repeat the call died in the conviction that I should be using breath to no purpose. Breath that I might be needing.

Suppression of the panic became increasingly tricky.

By allowing my mind to dwell for an instant on the situation, I risked creating a spiral of terror that would carry me beyond limits. I had to concentrate upon detail. Trivia. The kitchen equipment. Everything I could see was the finest, the costliest: nothing skimped, in line with Newstyle policy for the venture. These were going to be apartments for the discriminating purchaser, those who wanted something special, their own fragment of stately splendour, and were prepared to pay for it. As a further diversion I went over the estimated costs, so far as I could bring them to mind. No doubt inflation had outstripped them. But that was all right. We could simply ask more for the apartments, *pro rata*. No problem there. When I could discuss the matter with Albert we would run over the figures and fix upon a revised scale of charges. Albert had the building costs on tap.

The great selling point would be the seclusion. Half a mile from the nearest road, three miles from the Aylesbury outskirts . . . what jaded town-dweller could demand more while enjoying all the amenities of a serviced block? Children could run riot in the grounds: nobody would hear them. No traffic hazards. No intrusion from outside. Utter insularity.

Echoes apart, I knew there had been a reason for not repeating my shout.

Something about the bonds holding me seemed a little unusual. By dint of more neck-twisting I discovered what it was. Instead of being in direct contact with the flesh, the twine about my wrists and ankles had been padded out with foam rubber, as though to prevent abrasions. Even at the knees and shoulders, where my trousers and overcoat protected the skin, folded cloth had been used as extra protection.

The precaution seemed oddly at variance with the disregard for physical comfort that marked the rest of the operation. I tried giving it some stern thought, treating it as a puzzle, an abstract brain-teaser, nothing concerning me personally, merely cerebral exercise.

Foam rubber padding. Plenty lying around, probably, along with the building materials. Likewise rags.

So, whoever had tied me up had been faced with no shortage of equipment. Nor, apparently, of time. A great deal of meticulous care had evidently gone into the binding process.

Leaning my head to the right, I made an attempt to reach the nearest knot with my teeth.

The gap was impossible to bridge. The closest strand of twine passed under my shoulders: a contortionist would have found it a challenge, and I had always made my living in other ways. My legs were doubled, with the knees directly ahead of my chin and the calves lashed to the thighs. My hands were between them. No movement of the arms was possible: they were pinioned by the strands holding me to the cooker. It was all fairly scientific, merciless as an equation. Immobility times constriction equals cramp, equals nightmare.

Think constructively. Outside, it was daylight. So it must be seven in the morning, at least. Building contractors start work at eight.

In an hour or less, help would be on hand.

Sixty minutes. I could take it for that long.

Provided I kept my brain occupied. Mental distraction was the key. Without it, the impulse to struggle, to strain impotently against the unachievable would be overwhelming.

It was like trying not to bite on a toffee lump. The forces impelling me to do what I was desperate not to do were primitive, insistent. A kind of self-hypnosis was needed, and I had no skill in the art. All that sustained me was a subconscious horror of what I might do to myself if I let things slip. This, and the hope that my predicament was temporary.

The fact that I was parched was of secondary concern. The glistening chrome taps arched like swans' necks over the sinks were there to taunt me, but hunger and thirst I could live with. At home about this time, I should be making coffee. Not to quench thirst, but as an addictive self-injection. So what was I missing?

It came to me that I was perhaps assuming a lot. Conceivably, it was later than I had figured. The entire day might have slipped by: this could be the following evening, the light outside emanating from the sun not as it rose, but as it set. The workmen could have been and gone. They need have had no cause to enter the show flat. They would not have known I was there.

The cars would have meant nothing to them, either. Assuming they were still where we had left them, Albert and I, they could easily have been taken by each group of men as belonging to two from another.

And the probability was that they were no longer there. Whoever was responsible for my present condition and had spirited Albert away would have found no difficulty in driving both cars away out of sight. They could be hidden in stables somewhere. Buried in bushes. To anticipate help from that source was wishful thinking.

On the other hand, to speculate that a new night was imminent did little to help morale, and mine needed all the help it could get. Better to assume that I had been right the first time. I had now been conscious at least half an hour, and it had been daylight all that time; it could not be long before the contractors arrived to start work. They might even commence before eight. Thompson's, as Albert had said, were a good firm, packing a fair week's work into five days . . .

Five days.

It dawned on me then. Today, if I had it right, was Saturday. A non-working day. Thompson's men always took the weekend off. It would be Monday morning before they were back.

Two days. Two nights.

Two thousand, eight hundred and eighty minutes.

Suddenly my thirst was intolerable.

CHAPTER 12

It began to rain.

I could hear it thrashing against the window. The noise jerked me back from semi-trance, partly self-induced, partly the result of near-starvation. I couldn't tell how long I had been like that.

Midway along the wall to my left, an insulated cable-end protruded from a hole in the tiling. Its likely purpose was to feed an electric clock: no clock had yet been provided. My watch was concealed by my sleeve. Before the rain had returned I could hear the watch ticking but I couldn't expose the face. My hands were locked together.

A call of nature was beginning to cause me some slight discomfort. This suggested a sizeable lapse of time since my first awakening. Happily, the little fluid I had consumed lately meant that this particular problem was not too acute at present. If anything, I was edging towards dehydration, which in turn, I guessed, was contributing to drowsiness. With any luck, I should soon drift back into complete unconsciousness. Until Monday morning.

The kitchen wall-tiles were a vivid marriage of orange and green, flecked with black. They complemented the window-blind nicely. Someone had brought taste and imagination to the design. Rightly so. Important places, kitchens. The wives had a wary eye for them. And it was the wives who had the final say in the purchase decision. Market lore, this. Sell it to the little woman and you're home and dry.

As for the menfolk, they had an eye for the practical detail. This, at least, was the myth. Experience had led some of us to question it. Men, in a weird way, could be cloudier of vision, adrift in a world of dreams . . .

I awoke from a railway station.

I had been striving to catch a train, a curving serpent of inscrutable coaches alongside a platform separated from me by a barrier, a tall structure of steel and concrete which, to stand a chance of jumping aboard, I had somehow to surmount. To and fro I lumbered, seeking an opening. A newspaper vending kiosk kept impeding me. Try as I might, I found myself continually back in its vicinity, further than ever from the barrier, like Alice barred from her hill. My attempts to leap it were useless: I couldn't get off the ground. The train started to leave. I had a clear view of it, remarkably clear, as it snaked clear of the platform towards a network of points. It was heading for me. I was in the centre of the network, my feet trapped by the rails. The train's whistle screamed.

The rain had stopped. I had no feeling in my limbs.

In the dead silence of the kitchen, I wondered about that scream.

The question bothered me for some time. But at a low level, two or three on the Richter Scale of awareness; mere subterranean rumblings, masked by the surface pulsations of physical misery which gathered force with the return of sensation to my body. The numbness had crept away, yielding to pain of an intensity I could never have imagined. I began to sob.

Far from relieving me, every intake of breath was a bruising challenge to the twine, a kick in the ribs. And yet I was too weak to stop. I was getting perilously near the state I had dreaded—powerless to fight the instinct to squirm, struggle, pit my muscles uselessly against the cool invincibility of the cords. I was within nodding distance of lunacy.

When I awoke again, the crisis had passed.

As far as my position allowed it, my head had dropped forward, causing an outsized crick in the neck. A dull pain had lodged in the lower half of my spine, but my legs and arms were under sedation. This time I was careful. I thought of nothing. I visualized space, a purple void, and swam into it with eyes tightly shut. It wasn't too difficult. There seemed to be less competition from outside. Behind me, far behind, pain floundered in pursuit.

The sound thundered across the universe.

The Creation. I was there, in at the birth, a witness of the Big Bang. Cosmic moaning. A multitude of voices, lifted in animation. The universe shook.

'Steve?'

'Here,' I wept.

One side of the universe caved in, permitting encroachment. 'Hi there, old fellow. I expect you thought I'd forgotten you.' Albert stood gazing down at me. 'Good Lord. You look a sorry mess and no mistake. Was I longer than you'd expected?'

'I just hoped. Nothing else for it. Get me loose, for Christ's sake.'

'Just half a second.'

Turning, he placed something carefully on the working surface behind him before crossing to the window and checking the blind. His shoes made a comforting racket on the tiled floor. He still wore the anorak, but the hood now hung at the back. He looked fresh, unscathed.

'I'd have been back before,' he remarked, tweaking the blind an inch lower, 'only one or two things held me up. It's dark again now, did you know?'

'Still Saturday?'

'Oh yes. Weekend's only half over.'

'If you've got a knife handy . . . Can't stand this much longer.'

'No.' He regarded me intently. 'I don't suppose you feel that you can.'

'Look in one of the drawers,' I implored. 'There may be a knife. Or scissors.'

His head shook. 'There won't be.'

'How do you know?'

'We've kept the show flat clear of stuff like that.'

'Outside, then. I saw a workbench in the hall as we came in. Tools all round it.'

'That's an idea,' he said thoughtfully.

He stood tapping his fingers on the stainless steel drainer.

'Albo,' I said. 'I'm at the end of my tether. Jump to it, for God's sake.'

He leapt into the air, came down with feet apart, knees bent. 'Sir! At the double—Sir!'

I peered up at his eyes. 'What's the matter with you? Can't you see the state I'm in?'

'Clearly.' He nodded briskly. 'Very clearly indeed.'

The kitchen performed half a revolution. When it stabilized, he was in the same position except that his knees were no longer bent. His manner was detached, a little severe, with the touch of curiosity that I had registered before.

'For pity's sake,' I whimpered.

His head tilted. 'Sorry? Would you repeat that?'

He sank slowly to his haunches, and from there to a sitting posture on the floor with his back to the sink unit, so that we were on the same level.

'You must have guessed,' he said. 'I can't believe you'd no idea.'

'I don't know . . . Get me out of here.'

'Why should I do that? I've gone to enough trouble getting you in.'

'If this is some kind of joke, Albo, it's not appreciated. I'm in agony and I'm exhausted.'

'I can see that.'

'Sounds as if you're *enjoying* the sight.'

'Oh, I am. Let there be no mistake.'

He sat watching me.

'Either you're off your chump,' I said, 'or you're . . .' I lowered my voice. 'Someone else outside? You're having to sham?'

He smiled. 'No, Steve. Shamming, I'm pleased to say, is no longer called for. And a welcome change it makes, I can tell you.'

'I don't get it.'

'No, old buddy, you don't. Not tonight. You'll have to

deny yourself. Sorry about that.'

'Deny myself what?'

'The willing services of my lady wife. All good things come to an end, you know.'

The twine cut deeply into my armpits.

'Now I see.'

'He sees.' Albert rested his chin on the backs of his hands.

'You've every right to feel . . . the way you do.'

'Thank you so much.'

'We hoped you didn't realize. Tried to keep it under wraps.'

'Difficult, isn't it? Nearly as difficult as not *showing* that *I* realized. Hardship all round. Terribly fraught.'

'One of those situations, I'm afraid. If we'd known you had suspicions—'

'Oh, I didn't. Not at any stage. One minute I'd no idea: the next, it was obvious. Simply a question of proof.'

'How did you come by that?' He said nothing. 'Private detective, I suppose? God, how squalid.'

'Mm. To us fastidious types. Faintly amusing, though, in a kind of way. Partner spying on partner, having it off with partner. A genuine closed-shop enterprise.'

'I can't blame you for wanting revenge. Even though you can hardly accuse me of taking Mel away from you. You'd lost her already.'

'Oh really? That's fine, then. I drop a cheque in the street, you pick it up and cash it. No ethical problem there.'

'Aren't you over-simplifying things a little?'

'But then I'm a simple-minded chap, aren't I, Steve? Goofy old Albert, the office buffoon. If I have this tendency to see things in black and white, it's due to a regrettable colour blindness which prevents me picking out the dirty grey. Sorry.'

The silence of the kitchen surrounded us. I wanted

badly to wipe my face: it felt a mess. The rest of my discomfort was more bearable. At least I now had company. And the knowledge that Albert knew about Mel and me was somehow a relief. I had never cared for the subterfuge. By and large, the position had altered for the better.

'I'm glad,' I said quietly, 'we don't have to pretend any more.'

'Oh, *I'm* glad. They say fact is preferable to fantasy.'

'I suppose I asked for this. Take you long to set it up?'

'Actually, no. Once the idea had jelled, the logistics were surprisingly easy. This—' he waved a hand—'was already available, of course: it was just a matter of timing things to culminate at the weekend. And the initial yarn-spinning—a piece of cake. If you'll pardon the mixed metaphor. All that farrago about me meeting a girl called Jennifer at a concert, following her home, bumping her off . . . It sounded so daft, you believed it. Knowing your opinion of me, I estimated you would.'

'I had my doubts. But then you did take me to an actual place in Finchley and we did find an actual corpse . . . as I thought. Who was it, incidentally?'

'My father,' Albert said matter-of-factly. 'He was quite happy to help out.'

'Did he know exactly what you were up to?'

'I told him it was a spot of come-uppance for the seducer of my wife. That was enough for him. He still thinks highly of Mel.'

'On a point of strict accuracy,' I said, 'it was Mel who seduced me.'

He shrugged. 'Just as it takes two to make a quarrel . . . Well, we won't go into that. I was telling you about my arrangements. The Finchley apartment was the ticklish bit, but I had a stroke of luck there. You remember Frank Tapping? Works for an estate agency in Hampstead. I ran into him recently, and in course of conversation he happened to mention these Finchley properties they had on their books for holiday letting. The idea simply jumped in front of me.'

'You took a short lease of the place?'

'A friend did, on my behalf. A heavily disguised friend, I may say, using a false name. Once I had the key, I was able to set the wheels in motion. Need I say more?'

'I'd rather you took some action. Like cutting me out of this corset.'

'Not just yet.'

'You really are intent on rubbing my nose in it, aren't you? I can understand your feelings, Albert. No doubt I deserve penal treatment. In passing, though, I might point out that what you're doing is against the law. And isn't it a bit out of proportion? This can't be the first time a husband has had his place taken by a friend.'

'It's the first time it's happened to me.'

The low intensity of his response reduced me to silence. Biting the nails of his left hand, he was staring through the open doorway into the lobby, which from where I was shackled I couldn't see. Adjusting my muscles with caution, I winced as the twine issued a sharp reminder of its presence. Still observing the lobby, Albert said, 'Not too comfortable, Steve?'

'You've seen to that,' I said tautly. 'How much longer are you proposing to sit there, enjoying the sight of me?'

His brooding stare returned to my face. 'I can't say I enjoy the sight of you.'

I swallowed. 'If it's an apology you're waiting for, I might as well make one thing clear. I can't see that any purpose would be served.'

'I see.'

'These things happen. I do feel sorry about it, in a way. But to ask your pardon at this stage of the game would be slightly ridiculous, don't you agree?'

'If you say so.'

'I'll mouth a formula, if you like. If it would make you feel better.'

'Please don't bother.'

I met his eyes, glanced away, met them again. They had a hard brilliance that chilled my blood.

Preferring talk to silence, I said on a conversational note, 'That guy. The one who kept tabs on me yesterday and then called at my flat. Was he your private eye?'

'The very same.'

'An extra assignment. He must have done well out of you.'

'He's a good bloke,' Albert said pensively. 'Highly discreet, at the right price. A week after I hired him, he'd told me all I needed to know about the pair of you . . . every sordid detail. So when the time came, I used him again. Only this time I told him *not* to be discreet. He was to show himself as much as he could — really stand out in the crowd. Psychological pressure, you see. All part of the build-up.'

'It did get to me,' I admitted. 'I began to think I was hallucinating. That interview he had with me was brilliant. You'd primed him, of course?'

'The general outline. With special emphasis on the Finchley angle. The more we harped on that, I reckoned, the more alarmed you'd become.'

Another thought hit me suddenly. 'The phone calls. She spoke about Finchley, too. Who was she? Don't tell me you recruited your mother, as well?'

Heaving himself upright, he went to the door. A spike of fear pierced my stomach. 'You're not leaving?'

'Relax, friend.' He came back from the lobby. 'I just want to introduce Jennifer.'

A figure followed him into the kitchen. 'Hallo, Stephen,' said Amanda. 'Getting a little worked up, are we?'

CHAPTER 13

'He's looking dumbfounded,' remarked Albert. 'I can't quite see why.'

'Neither can I,' she agreed. 'It must have been obvious, ever since my performance for the benefit of the police.'

'But then, he's had a lot on his mind.'

'And still more on his body.' She inspected me with interest. 'Thorough job you made of that, Mr Hall. How long has he been like this?'

Albert made mental calculations. 'About nineteen hours.'

'Will he be able to move?'

'It'll hurt at first.'

'Good,' she said.

'I know what axe Albert has to grind,' I said from the floor. 'What's yours, Amanda? Don't I pay you enough?'

She looked down at me with a kind of disdain. Taking up his former position at the sink, Albert stood with folded arms, examining our secretary with grave approbation. 'Girls like Amanda,' he said, 'don't care to be taken for granted.'

'I'm sure, if I've ever given the impression—'

'You've given nothing. That's what she complains of.'

'No need to go on about it, Mr Hall.'

'Please, do go on. What the hell is this? Have I upset Amanda in some way?'

She lifted her gaze to the ceiling. Albert continued to inspect her like a Dutch uncle. 'Girls like Amanda,' he repeated, 'would do anything for anybody . . . but when they're kicked in the teeth, naturally they tend to snap.'

'Okay,' I demanded, 'so what have I done wrong? Did I offend her without realizing it?'

Amanda's gaze dropped. 'People like you,' she announced, 'wouldn't notice if they trod their own kids into the sand.'

'I'm baffled,' I said desperately. 'I can't seem to make sense of what you're saying, Amanda. If I've neglected your interests at any time, I regret it sincerely, I couldn't be more sorry, but I honestly—'

'I don't think,' she told Albert, 'I can listen to any more of this. I'll be next door.' Without another glance, she left the kitchen.

'Sensitive girl, Amanda,' observed Albert. 'Never appreciated that, did you, Steve?'

'Evidently not. What did I do, or fail to do?'

'She's also somewhat old-fashioned. In the light of which, your behaviour of the past year or so was hardly calculated to impress her. Not content with turning a blind eye to the fact that she cared for you, you had to go straight off and fornicate with my wife. Amanda can't forgive you for that.'

'Amanda?' I said incredulously. 'She had a thing about me?'

'It is slightly amazing. She can hardly credit it herself, now. Especially since she found solace in her religion.'

'Religion?'

'Been a great comfort to her, I believe. One of these fringe sects, a trifle rigid on the moral side and none the worse for that. Given her the anchor she was looking for. We all have to seek our own brand of consolation.'

'I trust,' I said through clenched teeth, 'you're both finding all you need at the moment.'

Albert mused. 'You may think,' he said presently, 'we're an unorthodox alliance, but Amanda's been very helpful to me . . . very supportive. And she's come up with an idea or two of her own, what's more. The mystery phone calls—that was one. I'd rather like to have heard those.'

'I'm sure you've both been pretty smart. But how could you possibly know I'd react in the way you wanted at the outset? When we found the "corpse" at Finchley, I might easily have insisted on reporting it straight to the police.'

'In which case, I'd have passed it off as a practical joke that got out of hand. But you didn't, did you? And I was reasonably confident you wouldn't. Why? I think you know the answer to that one.'

'Suppose you tell me.'

'If you insist. You didn't want the police involved because you were scared of the possible repercussions. If you'd refused to help me and I'd been charged with somebody's murder, who knows what I might have let slip, in my resentment? That was a chance you just couldn't bring yourself to take, eh, Steve?'

'I don't know what you're talking about.'

'Oh, come on. A little matter of . . . sorry, no, correction—one hell of a matter of tax evasion, stretching back over the years. Lynchpin of the Newstyle machine. On which I unluckily placed my finger eighteen months after joining the outfit, with the result that to keep me sweet you were obliged to deal me in on the racket. Not discussed it much since then, have we? Just left it to an amenable auditor to get on with, and pocketed the loot.'

'You were happy enough with the arrangement.'

'I don't deny it. I'm not claiming to have nursed scruples. But let's admit it, I *was* in a position to pull the plug out from under you if I chose.'

'Yourself as well.'

'Certainly. But if I was up on a murder rap and felt I owed you a grudge for not standing by me, I might not have been too choosey about what I blurted out. That's how you reasoned it, wasn't it, Steve? That's how I knew you'd reason it. And that's why I knew you wouldn't go to the police.'

'But I did, eventually.'

'Only when you thought I'd been disposed of. Which is when your troubles really started. I don't know about you,' said Albert, removing a coffee-mug from a hook and filling it at the tap, 'but in my opinion we orchestrated the whole thing beautifully, Amanda and I. That copper—what was his name? Johnson—must have ended up convinced he'd tangled with a real nut. Office delusions, disappearing partners, vanishing corpses . . . dear, oh, dear. He's probably still describing your symptoms to the divisional psychiatrist, and who could blame him? One antisocial act from you within the next week and he'll know he was right. By the way, are you thirsty?'

'Among other things.' My voice was starting to sound like rough wood grating on brass. I watched tensely as he approached with the mug. Lowering it to floor level, he pushed it to within a few inches of my right hip.

'I'll leave it there,' he said, returning to the sink. 'You can have a swig whenever you want.'

I stared up at him. 'I can't reach it.'

'No, neither you can. Never mind, it's only water, you're not missing much. Well now,' he said briskly, rubbing his hands together. 'Anything I haven't explained? We don't want you to feel uninformed on any aspect.'

'Albert—please cut me loose.'

'I'd offer you Scotch, but there's nothing drinkable on the premises. And I clean forgot to bring a bottle with me. Too much else to think about.'

'You bastard.'

'How was that, again?' His voice was soft.

'Look, you've got me just where you want me. You're enjoying it. You like seeing me squirm. Okay, I'm squirming. But it's been a night and a day. I've had it. Can't you—'

My voice failed. Trying to clear my throat, I achieved a dry barking sound that hurt the lining. 'Why don't we call it quits?' I rasped.

'A night,' he repeated slowly, 'and a day. You're lucky. I've had eleven months of nights and days. Nights, in particular.'

'No use harping on it, Albert. You won't bring her back.'

'Have you any conception of what it's like? A creature you've worshipped? Knowing she's in the arms of someone else . . . knowing you have to face that someone again, time after time, talk to him, smile at him, pretend you enjoy running a business with him? Wanting to smash his grinning face? Can you perform a mental somersault and picture the way I felt?'

'Yes, Albert. I can.'

'Yes, Albert, I can,' he mimicked, reproducing exactly the hoarseness of my utterance.

'How much longer?'

He regarded me silently.

The water glistened in the mug. Wanting to take my eyes off it, I couldn't. It hypnotized me. I craved to lean sideways, grip the mug's rim in my teeth, upend the contents into my throat. As my nerve-centre dictated the movement, my constricted sinew met crushing resistance. Panic welled once more, panic mingled with pain, self-pity, an incoherent rage. I shut my eyes. When I reopened them, the nightmare would have dissolved.

'You're not asleep,' said his voice. 'It's happening. You can't buy yourself out of this one, Stevie boy.'

'How do I make amends, then? Tell me.'

'No need to bother, old son. It's irrelevant.'

I reopened my eyes. 'Tell me one thing, Albert. Before leaving my flat last night to go to Finchley—before your private eye called on me, in fact—I'd phoned Mel and asked her to come over. She said she'd leave immediately. But she didn't arrive.'

Albert made a tutting noise.

'And yet,' I continued, hearing my voice as a wheeze inside my ears, 'when Sergeant Johnson and I got to your place she apparently wasn't there, either. You said she was playing bridge.'

'I'm used to keeping up appearances.'

'Have you seen her since then?'

'Actually,' he confided, 'I've been seeing a good deal of her.'

'What have you been up to, Albert? Where's Mel now?'

He strolled out of the kitchen.

'If you've done anything to her,' I yelled huskily, 'you'll live to regret it, I promise you.'

Impotently I heaved against the cooker. It felt about as yielding as Nelson's Column. Fury was building up inside me and there was no way I could give vent to it. Except verbally, and this I had to avoid. Nothing, I sensed, would have charmed Albert more than futile abuse. With the possible exception of snivelling appeals to his mercy. I hadn't yet reached this stage. It was wretchedly close, but as long as I could fend it off I was resolved to do so.

Amanda's complicity had come as a shock. Looking back, however, I now recalled things, scattered incidents that might have alerted me: her manner sometimes when, a year or two previously, she had brought me the morning mail or a cup of coffee, or was recounting some point made to her by a client . . . with someone else, I might well have clinched the connection. Amanda just hadn't seemed the type. In a dispassionate way, I had recognized that she possessed enough animal attraction to be leading, presumably, a life of her own beyond the office boundaries. But she had never spoken of boy-friends and I had never asked. She was simply Amanda, thirtyish and efficient. Never had I thought of her as I thought, day and night, of Mel.

There were other, more recent things that came back to me. Clicks on the line when Mel and I spoke on the phone. We had a coded system: she would call, ostensibly to talk to Albert but knowing he would be out, and would then be transferred to me for a subtle discussion of plans. After these conversations, now that I thought about it, there had been a tendency for Amanda to appear a little remote. Once or twice I had even ribbed her about it.

All right, I had worn blinkers. But I could hardly have been expected to guess that my secretary, thwarted in infatuation, would fall victim on the rebound to an attack of religious mania that would warp her outlook to the extent of teaming up with hate-laden Albert in a scheme like this. You read about such things in Sunday newspapers. They don't *occur* to people.

My own outlook was now under drastic review. However long or briefly the pair of them pursued their idiotic revenge, Newstyle Properties in its present form was finished. Once the immediate crisis was passed, some arrangement would have to be made for the inevitable split. Then there would be the divorce proceedings. Myself named as co-respondent. In turn, the civil suit that I should be bringing against both Albert and Amanda, claiming damages for abduction, unnecessary pain and suffering . . . whatever Rogerson, my personal solicitor, recommended as likely grounds for action.

It was all going to be exceedingly messy.

Thinking about it did little for my pulse count. So I forced my mind back to the current problem: that of persuading my tormentors that they had carried their bizarre retaliation far enough. Surely they were not contemplating keeping me here another night?

I hadn't cared for the look in Albert's eye.

Several minutes had elapsed since his sauntering departure from the kitchen. As far as I was aware, no doors had opened or shut during that time: were he and Amanda still in the apartment? Fear rushed back. I raised my voice to a croak.

'Anyone there? I think I'm going to pass out.'

Scuffing noises reached my ears. After an interval, I was presented with a rear view of the stooped figure of Albert as he backed through the doorway. He was breathing hard. Evidently Mel's weight was taking it out of him, albeit part of the burden was being borne by Amanda, who had a grasp of her legs. Without noticeable tenderness, they deposited her on the floor. She was clad in a short nightgown of transparent nylon under a fluffy green robe, open down the front. Her blonde hair tumbled around her shoulders. She was apparently asleep. The robe was one I didn't recognize. At my apartment, she had usually worn one of mine. When she bothered to wear anything.

Albert straightened, gasping a little. 'Company for you.'

'What have you done to her, you bloody savages?'

He looked mildly surprised. 'You asked where she was. We decided to show you.'

'Happy now, then? You've got us both here, nicely under control. What filthy dope did you use on her?'

'Same as you had in your coffee last night. Some exceptionally good stuff that Amanda contrived to lift from her first-aid class. Retribution,' he explained, 'out of the rates. As a tax evader, you'll appreciate the irony, Steve.'

'As an otherwise law-abiding citizen, I don't appreciate thuggery.' My lips felt arid and cracked. My tongue seemed too big for my mouth, like an unlubricated piston inside a cylinder. Painfully I added, 'How long have you been keeping her like this?'

'You're finding it hard to talk,' Albert said considerately, 'so let me explain. After you'd phoned my dear wife early yesterday evening and asked her to come over, she dutifully went straight down to our lock-up garage and got into her car. What she didn't know was that I'd beaten her to it . . . by several hours. In fact, I spent the entire afternoon in the rear seat with the newspapers, waiting for her to show up. As I knew she would. I knew you'd contact her about me, and that she'd want to drive over.'

Swallowing movements were made in his throat. Amanda sent him a glance.

'Needless to say,' he resumed, thrusting his hair back from his eyes, 'I hadn't gone in unprepared. Clever Amanda had got the chloroform for me—again from a beneficent college of further education—and when I heard Mel coming, all I had to do was soak the pad and wait. She never saw me. She was still putting the key in the ignition when I leaned over from behind.'

'You'd do that to your own wife?'

'Oh, she's mine, is she? Sorry, I hadn't realized. Well, I made up for it when she came round. She was pretty groggy and thought she'd been attacked by an intruder. So she was glad of the coffee I gave her, out of the flask I just happened to have with me. She's addicted to the stuff, as you well know.'

'How many tablets had you laced it with?'

'Sufficient. As soon as she was well asleep I shifted her to the back seat, locked up the garage, collected my own car from the nearby street I'd left it in and drove over to Finchley. After that, it was merely a question of waiting.'

'You couldn't have known. You couldn't have been sure I'd go there myself, the same evening.'

Albert conceded the point with a gracious gesture. 'I don't claim to be God. But there was one thing I knew for certain: at about the time I was dealing with Melanie, you were receiving a home visit from my faithful private eye, who had undertaken to talk to you mysteriously about Finchley. Well, think about it, Steve. In the circumstances, was it feasible that you'd be able to resist the urge to get over there later to find out what the devil was going on?'

'You were assuming a hell of a lot.'

'Yes, but there's something you're forgetting. We've known each other a long time, you and I. The difference between us is, you *think* you're well acquainted with my character, whereas I *know* I'm aware of almost every facet of yours. I've made a study of you, Steve. I know how your mind functions, how you're likely to respond to a given stimulus. I know that, fundamentally, you're a self-obsessed coward. What's more important—' he lobbed a faint smile in Amanda's direction—'I know very well your opinion of me.'

'I don't see what that has to do with it.'

'Think again. What made me spin you that incredible yarn about meeting a girl called Jennifer, pursuing her like some berserk Latin, taking insults from her at the most personal level? The fact that *I knew you'd never dream I could have made it up.* Pompous, egotistical, self-regarding . . . that's how you've always seen me—right, Steve? Dear old Albert, ever on his dignity. Last type in the world to tell a story against himself—unless it was true, and he felt he had to. So that's what I did. I concocted the thickest stew of fiction I could imagine the ingredients for . . . and you swallowed the lot.'

Once more, silence crawled into the kitchen and stayed there until Albert resumed his monologue.

'Just to round off the account . . . When I got to the Finchley place, I let myself in quietly and I didn't switch on any lights. I'd taken along a bottle of tomato sauce—yes, it was that easy—and I dabbed some on the back of my head plus a few drops over the floor. Then I arranged myself in the lifeless mass you found me in. I did have a few qualms about that particular masquerade. In the normal way, I doubt if it would have fooled anybody. But by that time, of course, you were well on the way to losing your nerve entirely. I was counting on that.'

'And his stupidity,' said Amanda.

'You'll note her current estimation of you. Well,

everything went largely as I'd anticipated. Away you dashed to call the cops. While you were gone, I cleaned myself up a little, wiped the spots off the floor, then drove back to my apartment, gave my hair a thorough rinse and blow-dried it. After that I settled down to await the arrival of you or the CID. As things panned out, it was both.'

He reflected. 'From then on, it all got progressively easier. Overall, I think we can say—can't we, Amanda?—we succeeded quite handsomely in our two main objectives. The first of which was to discredit you in the eyes of the law. Unless I'm much mistaken, you're now on official record as a raving paranoiac.'

'And the second?'

'To give you the fright of your nasty, self-centred life.'

'Mission accomplished,' I mumbled. 'Now can we all go home?'

Their eyes met. They exchanged a pair of smiles that turned my blood the rest of the way to ice.

CHAPTER 14

'Albert, can I just point something out?'

'By all means.'

I took a deep, painful breath. 'You're not the only pair involved. Bear in mind the others you've had to call on. Your own father . . .'

'He's a simple soul. More ingenuous even than me, Steve. I told him it was a prank and that's what he'll always believe. Anything that happens to you will be a bonus as far as he's concerned.'

'What about the private eye?'

'As I said, he's ultra-discreet. I've had dealings with him for a good while now—sadly—and I've learnt quite a bit about him. He's an ex-con who reckons he was framed by the police to serve a term, and he wouldn't pause to lift a finger if a constable lay bleeding in the gutter. On top of which, he's quite fond of money. His extra performances in the past couple of days have earned him a bomb. No, I don't think I've any qualms in his direction. Anyone else?'

'Amanda. You've got sense. Tell him.'

Albert uttered a quiet laugh. 'My good chap. Have you any conception how Amanda regards you? To those of her faith, adultery is the ultimate sin. People like you are germ-bearing insects, to be flattened underfoot.'

'You can't go through with it, Albo. All these years we've been together . . .'

'My God. Spare us that.'

He stood regarding me with his head to one side. 'First it was Clare. Merely an item in your collection, wasn't she, that young sister of mine? Useful for as long as she was amusing. Then, when you felt like better entertainment . . . You broke her heart, Steve. Did that ever occur to you?'

'Clare's married, for God's sake. With a family.'

'Yes, she makes a fair pretence of living. Then it was Melanie. Her, you took from me as casually as you might have accepted a coin for a phone call. You expect me to forgive you for that?'

'I expect rational behaviour. From one of you, at least.'

'You'll get it. Don't worry.'

I could no longer distinguish between the two of them. They had become simply a pair of giant motionless outlines, towering above me. Albert's voice came and went like the drone of a circling aircraft on a windy day.

'. . . leaving most of it to you . . . Listening, Steve? Your fingers on her throat . . . *Death Riddle of Couple in Rural Love-Nest*. Front-page news, Steve. *Property Whizz-Kid*

Strangles Mistress. Macabre Climax to Stormy Relationship . . .'

'Insane.'

'Yes. We rather think that's the conclusion the police will come to.'

'You'll overlook something. People always do.'

'No, no. Don't worry about that. We've covered everything.'

'Motive? How about that?'

'Beg pardon, old chap? You're getting awfully faint. Motive, you say? How does fear of exposure grab you? The tax fraud . . . you remember? Potential ruin. Your worried partner, suspecting the worst, had confided in his wife, who took it into her beautiful head to practise a spot of delicate blackmail on the side. Bleeding you for months, wasn't she, Steve? You had to be rid of her.'

'Sheer fantasy.'

'But you won't be on hand, will you, Steve, to explain that? My version will sound better. It would explain a lot about your recent behaviour.'

'You'll never carry it off.'

'Can't hear what you're saying. Don't jerk too hard, will you? We don't want your flesh bruised by the cords. Precautions were taken, as you may have noticed. However, I think now it's about time we . . . Ready, Amanda?'

'All set.'

' 'Bye then, Steve. I do hope the last forty-eight hours of your life were the worst you've ever spent.'

Amanda crouched over me. Holding the hypodermic to the light, she injected into the air experimentally before bringing the needle close, smiling into my face. 'This,' she said, 'will hurt quite a little.'

A cow lowed. It was answered by another.

Rural ululations.

Repeat the phrase rapidly, four times. Weird stuff, language. Infinitely adaptable. Inadaptably finite. Indubitably inadaptable. Rather like the mattress. Ridged in the wrong places. Poor design. Or shoddy workmanship. Too easy to blame management.

The cow mourned again.

Not noted for its cattle, the City of London. These must be strays. Fresh from Smithfield, perhaps. Let's get the hell out of here, one had said to the other, before we're so many raw joints. So off they had lumbered, keeping to the left, observing the traffic signals. Heading for the fields to avoid the slaughter . . .

I sat up.

The room was in semi-darkness. To the left was a window, a pale shade of sepia. Curtains, nearly drawn. The window was the wrong shape. It should be square, single-paned, a replica of six hundred others in the block. This one was almost rectangular, arched at the top, criss-crossed by small frames. How the hell had that happened during the night?

My head . . .

Clutching it, I sank back on to pillows with a groan that lasted all the way down.

A draught hit me. I felt chilled to the bone.

Why was I lying on top of the bedclothes?

In my underpants?

The watch face on my left wrist was just discernible. Six fifty, it said.

Suddenly the room became lighter. A weak beam of sunlight was responsible, hopping between the curtains to settle upon flock-papered walls. I turned my head.

She was lying next to me, face upwards, mouth open.

I said, 'Mel?'

Only nothing emerged. My lips formed the syllable, my lungs powered the larynx, to no avail. I tried again. It came as a kind of whistle, unrecognizable as speech.

Managing to lift myself again, I stared down at her. The hem of the nightgown had ridden up to her waist. She lay in a sprawl, one leg outflung to the edge of the bed. Her left arm rested across her stomach. Her white upper teeth gleamed in the window-light.

'*Christ.*' I rolled away from her. 'Bastard maniacs . . .'

I landed heavily on a carpeted floor. Rising from it was a challenge, a demanding exercise for limbs that felt filleted, prodded by a brain that seemed to have been washed in detergent and wrung out. When I did achieve a standing position, the room bucked and heaved like a ship's stern in a force ten gale. Averting my eyes from the bed, I pitched myself in the direction of the door, five miles to my left. Toddlerlike, my knees splayed and buckled, and I fell over.

Hoisting myself up, I took a new sighting on the door and reeled towards it.

I was vaguely puzzled to find it unlocked. Outside, the lobby was illuminated by an unshaded standard lamp in one corner. Its beam highlighted a large square of plain white card that was attached with Sellotape to the wall facing me. The card bore a message in black ink, or paint.

HI, SUCKER. HOPE YOU FOUND IT A ROCKY RIDE. SEE YOU IN THE DIVORCE COURT.

I stood looking at it for a long time.

When I finally returned to the bedroom, Mel was in the same position except that her mouth was less wide open. Leaning across, I placed a hand against her cheek. It was warm. I took a grip of her shoulders and shook her, hard.

The mattress bounced beneath us. Riding with the motion, she remained oblivious, but I heard a sound, the tiniest of sighs, and I went on shaking in a kind of frenzy until I was exhausted. Then I got off the bed and went to the window and looked out.

The parkland looked superb. Under the dawn sun its

turf and broadleafed trees meandered across the undulating acres, losing themselves in a hazy distance. Momentarily at least, the bad weather had blown itself out. Away to the right a few cows, released from winter quarters, could be seen sampling the pasture. Beyond them in a hollow, the surface of a small lake sparkled like a platinum brooch.

Albert had been right. Pendover Manor had the look of a winner.

Part of the gravel drive could also be seen from the window, and the tail end of my car was just visible. The Lancia had gone. Having satisfied myself on this score, I returned to the bed and started shaking Melanie again. After about five minutes she began shaking her head, moaning softly, trying to push me away. I was persistent. When she was sufficiently roused to show signs of wanting to rearrange her limbs in more decorous positions I went away to the kitchen, filled the two coffee mugs with icy water, took them back and threw it over her. She sat up with a gasping shriek. Then, like me, she groaned and clutched her skull.

I said, 'I know how you feel. It'll pass off.'

With her, it took longer. I had found my outer clothes bundled on a chair, and I was now fully dressed but still shivering. While she took her first faltering steps around the bedroom I went back to the lobby and tore the card from the wall. Opening the outer door, I hunted about the tool-strewn entrance hall until I came across a metal wheelbarrow parked in an alcove. Placing the card inside it, I applied a match to one corner, held it vertical until it flared, dropped it back, watched it blaze for a moment. Even a non-smoker could find a use for a match. I always carried a small box as a social precaution.

Looking dazed, Melanie was sitting on the edge of the mattress, wrapped in the eiderdown. She said, 'I'm cold.'

'Me too.' The window, I had discovered, had been left

three inches open, top and bottom, to circulate the air nicely. Melanie's teeth chattered. Removing my overcoat, I said, 'Put this round you instead. We're leaving.'

'Where the hell are we?' Her enormous eyes were still dull, although behind them I could detect traces of the imperious spirit of the woman to whom Albert had been ill advised enough to enslave himself. She didn't look attractive to me this morning. I wondered whether she ever would again.

'Tell you on the way home. It'll be warmer in the car.'

'This isn't your place,' she said querulously. 'I don't remember coming here. I don't remember much at all. God, my head.'

'There's quite a lot to explain.' I took her by an arm. Mechanically she held the overcoat together around her.

'My clothes . . . ?'

'That's part of the explanation. Move as fast as you can. Another half-hour of this place and we'll both be dead from pneumonia.'

'I wish I knew where we are,' she complained.

'You'll find out,' I assured her. 'I've a feeling we're going to be shown some revealing photographs in due course.'

I wondered, without much caring, who would have handled the camera: Albert himself, or the clever Amanda, revealing yet another talent. Or Padded Jacket, possibly, earning himself a little extra. The point wasn't important. Doubtless it would be clarified when the time came. I had more immediate things on my mind.

At my urging she preceded me out of the bedroom, through the lobby and into the entrance hall. She was still tottery on her feet. Several times she half tripped and I had to support her. Midway across the hall I remembered something. I said, 'Wait here a moment.'

Leaving her standing near the workbench, on and around which a variety of tools had been left in careless profusion, I made a diversion to the alcove to inspect the wheelbarrow. A film of black flakes covered the base. To make certain, I stirred them with my fingers. The card had been entirely consumed. I tipped the wheelbarrow on to its side.

As I did so, a noise came from behind me.

I spun in time to see it happen. Losing her balance, Melanie had fallen heavily against the workbench. Flailing a hand for support, she grabbed at the nearest object, which happened to be one end of a bow-saw. The other end bounced on the bench-top, and the implement sprang three feet into the air.

I shouted, 'Watch it!'

It came down blade first, across her throat.

They tell me I could get off with manslaughter by claiming an accident. Alternatively, a plea of diminished responsibility might be worth trying. Those representing me seem to favour the latter course in the light of police enquiries, having particular regard to the testimony of Detective-Sergeant Johnson. I have tried to explain. It was indeed, I have told them, the sheerest accident, stemming from Melanie's own action and no other. Unassisted by a dignified silence from my partner and my secretary, I have done my utmost to counter the general hostility by pointing out that of course my fingerprints were found on the handle of the bow-saw, since I was the one who had dragged it off her; and further, that it had been neither my wish nor intention to spend a country weekend with her in the first place. I have also been at pains to dispute the suggestion that, having regard to her blackmailing propensities and my own vulnerability in this respect, our relationship had started to prey on my mind, inducing eccentric and, ultimately, deranged and destructive behaviour.

It does, of course, represent a way out. Of sorts. But

I'm damned if I'm going to be treated as an imbecile. Somehow, I intend to find a way of convincing everybody of the accuracy of my own account.

I must admit, though, I'm having no success at the moment.

Dodge City Public Library
Dodge City, Kansas